Wycliffe and the Beales

By W. J. Burley

Wycliffe and the Beales

W. J. BURLEY

PUBLISHED FOR THE CRIME CLUB BY
DOUBLEDAY & COMPANY, INC.
GARDEN CITY, NEW YORK
1984

All of the characters in this book
are fictitious, and any resemblance
to actual persons, living or dead,
is purely coincidental.

Library of Congress Cataloging in Publication Data

Burley, W. J. (William John)
Wycliffe and the Beales.

I. Title.
PR6052.U647W87   1984   823'.914
ISBN: 0-385-19189-8
Library of Congress Catalog Card Number 83–25364
First Edition in the United States of America

To my sister, Edith.

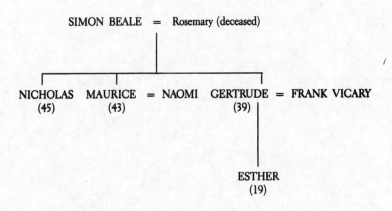

SIMON BEALE = Rosemary (deceased)

NICHOLAS   MAURICE = NAOMI   GERTRUDE = FRANK VICARY
(45)   (43)   (39)

ESTHER
(19)

Also EDWARD, Simon's nephew by marriage
(21)

Wycliffe and the Beales

Chapter One

Bunny Newcombe must have had a proper first name but even contemporaries who had been at school with him had forgotten what it was. He had lived all the forty-four years of his life in a cottage on the outskirts of the village and for several months, since the death of his mother, he had lived there alone. On leaving school Bunny had started out as a rabbit catcher but myxomatosis had put an early stop to that and so he had drifted into casual work around the village and on neighbouring farms. In the weeks and months following his mother's death he had grown to look more and more like a tramp, his skin had acquired a smooth patina of ingrained dirt and he was rarely seen without a greyish stubble on his chin and upper lip. Recently, too, he had shown less interest in getting work and this had led to the belief that his mother must have left him some money.

Bunny knew and was known to everybody but he had no close friends; he spent his evenings at the village pub where he was as much at home as the landlord, and the last evening of his life was passed like any other. He sat in his corner near the bar, drank his usual ration; then, at a little before half past ten, he emptied his final glass, wiped his lips with the back of his hand, and got to his feet. He was rarely drunk but by this time of night he had had enough.

" 'Night, all!"

A chorus of goodnights followed by a general laugh. Bunny was tolerated; a kind of mascot. He was barely five feet four in height with the proportions of a barrel. He walked with deliberate, waddling steps to the door and out in the night.

Outside, he paused to accustom himself to the relative darkness and to the fresh, moist moorland air, then he crossed the Green, passed the tall iron gates of Ashill and turned off to his right down a narrow lane which had the high brick wall of Ashill estate on one side and trees on the other. Although it was a clear night with a half moon, it was dark under the trees but his steps never faltered and he plodded on like a tired old horse returning to stable.

Bunny rarely indulged in abstract thought and by late evening he was incapable of much organized thinking of any sort; his consciousness was sufficiently engaged with present sensations, with random samples from a rag-bag of memories, and with vague anticipatory longings and resolves. At this present moment he was thinking that he wanted to pee, that it would be a relief to get his boots off and drop into bed, that nobody had ever made a rabbit pie to equal his mother's.

But as a background to these immediate preoccupations his mood was euphoric; Bunny was convinced of a future very different from the past, a feeling which he summed up in the words "I'll show the bastards!" And these words he muttered to himself from time to time like a charm.

Another couple of hundred yards and he came to Quarry House, an oddly elegant little house where the Gould sisters lived—twins in their late thirties, who dressed alike and held themselves aloof from the villagers. Bunny, stung by the memory of a recent encounter, muttered again, "I'll show the bastards!"

From this point he could hear the steady, muffled roar of the waterfall in the grounds of Ashill; a sound which had provided a constant background to his whole life from that very instant when his ears had first opened to the world about him.

Not far from the Goulds' house there was a seat, dating from a time when the parish council had shown a passing interest in the lane. It was too dark to see the seat or anyone on it at all clearly but he could hear whisperings and chucklings. He called out, "You watch yourself, Nancy Gratton, or you'll need re-bushing before you drag 'im into church!"

A boy's voice came out of the darkness, clear and without rancour, "Get 'ome you ol' flea-bag an' mind your own business!"

From that point the lane descended more steeply, its surface broken by winter frosts and scoured by rains. A few more yards and, clear of the trees, he could see his own cottage, its whitewashed walls standing out in the moonlight.

He unlatched the gate which screeched on its hinges and entered the yard. Small scuffling noises came from rabbit hutches against one wall and he said aloud, "Goodnight, my beauties!" He lowered the flap on the hen-house where the birds had gone to roost, attended to his own needs in an outside privy, then let himself into the cottage by the back door. He passed through a lean-to scullery to the kitchen in almost total darkness but there he struck a match and lit a candle he had left standing on a corner of the table. The scene came to flickering life; the big square table littered with saucepans, dishes, cans, bottles, and packets; a dresser with only a few oddments of china left on the shelves; a window with a curtain dragged across it, sagging in the middle.

Bunny had an uncomfortable moment as it occurred to him what his mother would have said and done had she come back to find such squalor. But his mother would never come back—she couldn't; she was dead. Bunny bolstered his ego with another "I'll show the bastards!" Then he took the candle and, holding it high in front of him, climbed the steep, narrow stairs. As his head came above the level of the upper floor he experienced a vicious jab of stunning pain which shot through his skull; he lost consciousness, staggered, and fell backwards down the stairs. As he fell, life deserted the little fat man and there began at once those complex changes which would ultimately restore his body to Mother Earth. Bunny had died in the cottage where he had been born and where he had spent the forty-four years of his relatively untroubled existence.

Another balmy spring day, with Nature propagating in indecent haste. Wycliffe and his wife had spent most of their weekend in the vegetable garden, for this was the year when Helen had made up her mind on self-sufficiency in vegetables and soft fruit. Given a completely free hand she might have acquired an adjoining field and extended her activities to include a goat or two, even a Dexter cow; but he set the limit of animal husbandry at one fastidious and condescending cat who considered that he contributed more than his share to the commonwealth merely by being there.

Now it was Monday morning but Wycliffe found that the feeling of mellow tranquillity lingered, though his hands were scratched and galled. It was the slim file of weekend reports and the little bundle of interoffice memoranda on his desk which seemed unreal. He had difficulty in concentrating his attention; his eyes kept straying to the window where he could glimpse the tops of silver birch trees on the far side of the highway, their leaves breaking out in a greenish haze against the blue of the sky.

It was not long since he had refused to be considered for the post of deputy chief constable, soon to fall vacant. He had no regrets; the job would have cut him off from the kind of police work which gave him most satisfaction, and saddled him with more administration, which he loathed. But the fact remained, he was now at the top of his particular tree, and there he would stay for the rest of his career in the force. There was something definitive and final about the thought which made him vaguely depressed whenever it entered his mind.

Back to reality—reality in the shape of reports of all serious or potentially serious crime in the two counties. A quiet weekend, nothing to get worked up about: a couple of muggings, but against that, the mugger had been caught; half a dozen break-ins, a "domestic" involving G.B.H. . . . He turned to his mail but the telephone rang. "Wycliffe."

Information Room reporting a 999-call from a member of the public in the village of Washford: "A chap known as Bunny Newcombe has been found dead in his cottage where he lived alone. The village postman found him; he's been shot through the head. No weapon at the scene."

"A shotgun wound?"

"Not according to the postman who seems to know what he's talking about."

"You've notified Newton subdivision?"

"Mr. Kersey is on his way to Washford now, sir."

Kersey, newly appointed detective inspector, was beginning his apprenticeship out in the sticks as senior C.I.D. officer in a large rural subdivision based on the market town of Newton. After fifteen years as a city "jack" he was now finding out what it was like to live with straw in his hair.

Half an hour later Information Room called again. Kersey had confirmed the report by radio and requested assistance in what he believed to be a murder inquiry.

Wycliffe gave routine instructions; there was no need for him to be involved at this stage but on such a morning the office was poor competition. He called in his personal assistant: "I shall be in Washford if you want me, Diane."

Diane looked reproachfully at the unopened mail and at the little pile of interdepartmental memoranda. "When will you be back?"

"I've no idea!" He said it with the bravado of a rebellious school-boy.

Washford was twenty miles away in a fold of the southern moor, a village of granite and slate which looked as though it had grown out of the moor itself and, in a sense, it had. The centre of the village was the Green, bordered by the pub, the school, the church, and Ashill—home of the Beale family. A single street bisected the village, known as North Street above, and South Street below, the Green.

Wycliffe drove up South Street from the Newton road and parked with other cars near the church and under the beeches which fringed the Green. One of the parked vehicles was a police patrol car and there was an officer on radio watch. Opposite the church a smug Regency house with an ironwork balcony was set back behind a high wall and only visible through tall wrought-iron gates.

As Wycliffe got out of his car his first impression was of silence; the village had a *Mary Celeste* air. He had grown up in such a village —not in the West Country, but where the Black Mountains trail their skirts over the Welsh border into Herefordshire, and what he remembered most about his village was this silent stillness. Then he heard the shrill voice of a woman teacher through the open windows of the nearby school; a little later he became aware of the stream which slid swiftly by in its culvert with a continuous ripple of sound, and now and again came the "ping" of a shop doorbell.

The constable on radio watch directed him: "Down the lane by

Ashill, sir. You pass a funny little house on your right; keep on for another couple of hundred yards and you come to a cottage—a tumbled-down sort of place—you'll find Mr. Kersey there, sir."

"Isn't Ashill the Beales' place?"

"That's right, sir. Simon, the old man, lives there with all the family as far as I know."

Beales' Household Stores, an old established family business with branches in several towns. A few years back, the firm had taken on a new lease of life with the complete rebuilding of their store in the city centre and the opening of several cash-and-carry depots strategically scattered over the two counties. Wycliffe had met old Simon a couple of times at civic soirées.

Unknowing, Wycliffe followed in the footsteps of Bunny Newcombe. He had the high wall of Ashill gardens on his right and a screen of beeches on his left; the trees arched overhead, filtering the sunlight. He could hear the rippling of the stream close at hand and the more distant sound of a waterfall or mill-race. Where the wall came to an end there was a small pink house with white woodwork and dormer windows—like a doll's house—with *Quarry House* on the gate. To that point the lane was well surfaced and maintained, but beyond, it degenerated into a rutted track, fatal to the suspension of any vehicle less robust than a farm tractor. But the white walls of Newcombe's cottage were in sight.

The cottage must certainly have been recorded in the doomsday book of some council official as "substandard" or, more probably, "unfit for human habitation." No electricity, no piped water, no proper sanitation, not even a road. . . . Its whitewashed walls supported a roof where thatch had been replaced by corrugated asbestos, itself now green with moss. The backyard, with its collection of rural junk, reminded Wycliffe of the backyards of his childhood; a rusting milk-churn, part of a chain-harrow, a broken cartwheel and the inevitable mangle . . . with nettles growing up through it all. There was a sentry-box privy, and a hen-house in which the hens clucked in protest against their confinement; there were hutches where rabbits shuffled and thumped, demanding to be fed. . . . Somebody would have to see to the livestock.

Kersey was standing at the door of the cottage with a uniformed constable. A plank on bricks had been laid across the yard to avoid disturbing or effacing traces which the killer had almost certainly not left.

"The local G.P. has certified death," Kersey said. "He didn't have much option. Now we're waiting for the pathologist. This is P.C. Miller, sir, community officer for the subsection."

A constable with several years' service and a soft tongue to turn away wrath; immaculately turned out, shop-window of the force.

"Let's have a look."

The lean-to with its stone sink and pump, then the kitchen, so dimly lit that he had to wait for his eyes to accommodate; a sickly smell of decaying food and a buzzing of bluebottles; a littered table, a dresser with remnants of crockery on its shelves, a cooking range and a few kitchen chairs. Newcombe's body lay in a heap at the foot of stairs which led to the rooms above. His eyes were open and glazed over; his cap had fallen off and was lying on the floor. He was almost bald and the whiteness of his scalp contrasted oddly with the weather-tan and grime on his forehead and face. The wound of entry was neat and round but the bullet must have torn its way out. A hand-gun, fired at fairly close range. Odd, that! When rural tensions explode into shooting the weapon is almost always a shotgun. And this little man who looked like a tramp—why would anyone want to shoot him anyway?

Wycliffe had no idea of the trouble he would have finding an answer to that one. He returned to the backyard, to Kersey and the constable.

"I gather the postman found him?"

Kersey nodded. "Newcombe didn't have much post but whenever the postman did call he would find him here in the yard, feeding his rabbits. This morning, with the hens still shut up and nobody about he wondered if Bunny had been taken ill, so he opened the door and called out."

"The door wasn't locked?"

"No, but that doesn't mean much, they don't go in for locking up round here, apparently."

People hadn't locked their doors in Wycliffe's village either.

"Of course the postman went in and found him."

Wycliffe turned to the constable. "Do you know anything of the dead man?"

Miller was flicking whitewash off his uniform with a handkerchief. "I knew him pretty well, sir. He was the village odd-job man but he hasn't done much lately—not since his mother died. Occasionally he would lend Sammy Pugh a hand in his scrap-yard down on the Newton road. Sammy is a rogue; he was nicked for receiving, a couple of years back, and I wouldn't put it past Newcombe to turn a dishonest penny if he got the chance, but nothing on any scale; nothing organized."

"Yet somebody shot him."

Wycliffe got a cautious sidelong glance from the constable. "Yes, somebody did, sir, but I can't think who would want to or why."

"Any relatives or close friends you know of who should be told?"

Miller eased the strap of his helmet. "The only relative I know of is an aunt—a Mrs. Fretwell, she's the wife of our local builder and undertaker and I think she's his father's sister. As to friends, I don't think he had any; he was a loner."

Wycliffe said, "See his aunt and make sure she knows what's happening. Ask her if there are any other relatives."

A sound of cars farther up the lane and a little later Sergeant Smith arrived with his photographic gear and three detectives from Wycliffe's headquarters squad. Dr. Franks, the pathologist, followed almost at once.

Franks, bald and shiny as ever, greeted Wycliffe with his usual bonhomie and was taken into the kitchen.

"God! This place stinks. I can't do much with him here, that's for sure."

He waited while Smith took a series of shots from different angles, then made his preliminary examination.

"Not much I can tell you, Charles, that you can't see for yourself. He was shot, probably at a couple of feet, with a hand-gun; the bullet passed through his head carrying with it some of his brains and making a mess on the stairs. He's been dead between twelve and fifteen hours, I should think."

Franks looked about for somewhere to wash his hands and finding nowhere wiped them on a white linen handkerchief. "Of course, other features may turn up in the course of the P.M. but who wants other features with a hole in the head?"

Franks retreated into the yard and the sunshine and looked around with acute distaste. "The amenities of rural life I can do without, Charles. Be a good chap and get him over to me sharpish; I had plans for today."

Kersey said, "The van is here; the driver managed to back up off the Newton road. I only hope he can get away again without busting his back axle."

Soon Newcombe's body would be taken away to be subjected to the final indignity of a post-mortem. His cottage would be searched from top to bottom; surfaces carrying several months' accumulation of dust would be meticulously examined for prints and suddenly, a dead match, a cigarette end or a muddy footprint could acquire absurd importance. Detectives would tramp around the village questioning people about Bunny's habits, his foibles and his vices, his friends and his enemies—like journalists ferreting out the private life of a Royal. All this for a little fat man who had been of no importance whatever while he lived.

Sometimes, in a mood of disillusionment, Wycliffe saw the whole routine as macabre. The protection of Society—that was what it was about; not about the little man who never washed and had lived in squalor with only his rabbits and chickens for company. He had no more importance dead than alive except as a pointer to his killer.

Franks said, "I'll be off then." He went out of the yard, leaving the gate open, and a minute or two later they heard the roar of his Porsche as the wheels skidded on the rutted surface. The incongruous row died away and Kersey said, "Are you staying, sir?"

"For the present." He felt irritable and wondered why; then he realized that he was offended by Franks's boisterous professionalism —really by his total lack of interest in the dead man who, as far as Franks was concerned, was just another carcass to be probed and dissected. Complete detachment; a job of work. But wasn't that the proper, the correct attitude? All the same . . .

Newcombe was carried away on a stretcher, enveloped in a polyethylene sheet. His body was placed in the van and the van edged off down the lane, bumping over the ground and bouncing on its suspension. Exit Bunny Newcombe; the work could begin. Two men began to search the yard for those unconsidered trifles which are supposed to be the stuff of evidence. Wycliffe stood in the kitchen; he noticed that both drawers of the dresser were open and their contents had been scattered on the floor. Did this mean that someone had searched the place or that Newcombe had become irritated when looking for something he couldn't find?

There was a parlour on the ground floor which Wycliffe had not yet seen; he went in and, to his surprise, found it perfectly habitable —evidently as Bunny's mother had left it, except for dust. The chiffonier, like the dresser in the kitchen, had its drawers open, though their contents had not been tumbled on to the floor. There were photographs on the walls: two sepia prints on glass of seaside scenes in red-plush frames, and a large photograph in a black frame of a plump young man with a Charlie Chaplin moustache. He stood beside a good-looking girl who was seated; she wore a two-piece costume and a high-crowned hat. Bunny's parents?

One picture was missing, though the nail on which it had hung was there, so was the rectangular patch of wallpaper less faded than the rest. Wycliffe found the frame and the broken glass on the floor, apparently kicked aside, but the picture itself was not there. Oddly, the hanging cord was intact so it had not fallen from the wall.

A little window with net curtains looked out on a wilderness which had once been a garden. There were apple trees smothered in blossom, their trunks and boughs encrusted with grey-green lichens, and the grass and nettles were waist-high.

Newcombe, it seemed, had been the village jack-of-all-trades. In the past every village had one, just as every village had an idiot; an obliging girl who, for greater convenience, wore no knickers; and a tough guy who had spent a few months in gaol for beating some-body up. . . . But such people do not get themselves shot—or, if by some mischance they do, then the weapon is a shotgun and there is no mystery about it.

Wycliffe returned to the kitchen; this was where Newcombe had squatted since his mother's death; as a tramp squats in a cave, a deserted hut, or under a bridge. He had continued to sleep upstairs, for there were no signs of bed or bedding in the kitchen, but in time he would, no doubt, have contracted his world to the compass of this single room, and the rest of the house would have ceased to have any meaning for him. Wycliffe could not explain this need to encapsulate, to concentrate one's resources and responsibilities, though he could imagine something of the kind happening to him if he were ever left quite alone.

At any rate he was intrigued, and he poked around the smelly, squalid room with more than professional interest.

Finally he climbed the stairs which still bore sinister evidence of the manner of Bunny's end. There were two rooms upstairs, separated by a thin wooden partition, papered over. Here, too, one of the rooms—the front one with a large brass bedstead, was habitable while the other, little more than a cupboard, was just big enough for a single bed. Yet it was here that Newcombe must have slept; the pile of tumbled and grimy bedding testified to that. There were no drawers or cupboards in the smaller room but in the larger one, part of the contents of both wardrobe and chest of drawers had been turned out in heaps on the floor.

The impression of a search was inescapable but Wycliffe was unconvinced; the evidence had a contrived look, as though someone in a hurry had wanted to convey the idea that a search had been made.

He stood on the little landing, where he could see into both rooms. Bunny's mother, like his own, had had a fondness for framed photographs and there were four or five hanging on the walls of the larger room. One of them could have been of Bunny—a leaner Bunny, at fifteen or sixteen. He was reminded of the empty frame and broken glass on the floor downstairs; that too seemed to have something deliberate and contrived about it. Was he imagining things?

Heavy footsteps on the stairs, and D.C. Fowler's grey head emerged from the stairwell. "Is it all right to start up here, sir?" Fowler looked with distaste into the cubby-hole where Newcombe had slept. Wycliffe left him to it and went downstairs, out into the yard. More of his men had arrived and Kersey was briefing them for inquiries in the village. They were being watched by a fair girl in a pink, short-sleeved dress; she was looking over the low wall which separated Newcombe's place from the woods belonging to Ashill.

Wycliffe went over to her. "Do you want to tell us something?"
She looked at him, her face serenely solemn. "No."

"Do you mind telling me who you are?"

"My name is Vicary—Esther Vicary. I live in the house." She
nodded vaguely in the direction of Ashill house. "Have they ransacked the cottage?"

"Who are *they*?"

"Whoever killed him."

There was something unreal about the girl; her features and her
complexion were perfect yet totally lacking in animation so that one
had the impression of a beautiful mask.

"What makes you think the cottage might have been ransacked?"

"I wondered. The villagers pretend to believe that his mother left
him a lot of money—you know the sort of thing, hidden under the
mattress or up the chimney."

"You say they pretend to believe—don't they really think she had
money?"

"No. They say these things to make it more interesting but somebody might have thought it was true. I can't think of any other
reason for killing him."

She was eighteen or nineteen, older than he had first supposed,
self-possessed and cool, yet somehow childish; an odd blend of so-
phistication and naïvety. She spoke slowly and with a precision of
enunciation which matched the perfection of her features but without emphasis and without expression. Helen would probably have
spotted that her dress came out of the Laura Ashley stable; Wycliffe
thought it had an old-fashioned charm so that she looked like a
figure from an Impressionist painting.

He was puzzled by her. "You knew Newcombe well?"

"I've known him all my life." Unexpectedly she went on: "Do
you want someone to look after his rabbits and chickens?"

"Will you do it?"

"I don't mind for a day or two; I'll come back this afternoon,
when I've changed."

"Have you ever been inside the cottage?"

"I used to go there quite often when his mother was alive but I
haven't been there since. I expect it's in a state now."

"Do you remember the photographs on the wall in the parlour?"

"Not especially. I know there was a big one of his father and mother. Emily was very proud of it."

"Emily?"

"That was his mother's name—I used to call her by it because she worked at Ashill and everybody used her first name."

Wycliffe persisted. "There were three other photographs on that wall; two were seaside scenes in red-plush frames, the third had an oak frame with a gilt border—do you remember that one?"

"I'm afraid not—why?"

"It's not important."

She went off and Wycliffe watched her go.

The girl intrigued him; she had the slim asexuality of girls in Egyptian tomb paintings yet he caught himself imagining her nude; small, hard buttocks, slim boyish hips, tiny breasts. . . . Then he felt guilty because a Methodist upbringing still laid claim to his conscience. He could not make her out; sophisticated yet naïve; sexy yet sexless; detached yet apparently concerned . . . enigmatic, that was the word.

Smith brought him back to earth. "We've found the cartridge-case, sir, and Edwards has dug the bullet out of the lath and plaster at the top of the stairs. Nine-millimetre Parabellum; a foreigner—Italian, I think."

Which might tell ballistics something about the gun which fired it. Occasionally scratches on the cartridge-case made by the ejector mechanism will identify the breed of gun. In any case there was a routine response: "Check the register and bring in any nine-millimetre automatics. Start with this subdivision and see how we go."

There wouldn't be many; a nine-millimetre is a weapon for professionals—soldiers, policemen and hit men.

His detectives had finished in the yard so he released the hens, who rushed about madly, clucking and pecking, unable to come to terms with their belated freedom. He found an old oil drum half full of corn and scattered some for them.

The boundary wall where he had seen and talked to the girl was low in one place with flat stones built in to form a crude stile. He climbed up, standing on the wall; the sound of the waterfall seemed louder, but all he could see was a path disappearing into the trees, oaks and beeches being shouldered out by burgeoning sycamores.

He called to Dixon, who was working in the lean-to, "Tell Mr. Kersey I'll see him later," and dropped down on the other side of the wall. The path was overgrown but easily passable and after following it for a hundred yards he came out of the trees to a clearing which had been planted with rhododendrons and laurels, now running wild. On his left, a scrub-covered slope led down to a large pool, almost a lake, in what had once been a quarry; and ahead of him, from yet higher ground, the waterfall plunged out of a clump of trees to drop thirty feet or more to the pool. Although the volume of water was probably not large, the fall was impressive. A zigzag path broken by occasional steps led up from the clearing to a little pavilion in oriental style which bridged the stream at the point where it plunged over the edge, and there was a veranda which actually projected over the fall. A spot of chinoiserie in landscaping, which looked as though it had been lifted whole from a willow-pattern plate. A folly almost certainly antedating the Beales.

He climbed the zigzag path by the waterfall. From the top the way led on, presumably to the house, but on his left was the faded, red-painted door of the little pavilion. Out of curiosity he tried the handle and the door opened. The building consisted of a single room, furnished with a large table, three or four wicker chairs, a sofa which had once been upholstered in red plush, and a number of cupboards built against one wall. A latticed window and another door opened onto the veranda. A novel summer-house.

Dead leaves which must have blown in were scattered on the floor and there was dust everywhere. Faded photographs cut from *Picture Post* were stuck to the walls. He crossed the room and went through the second door to the veranda. It was an odd sensation to look over the low balustrade along the gleaming sheet of water, down to the foaming arc where it hit the surface of the pool. He was startled by the feeling of vertigo which gripped him, quite disproportionate to the drop, and he turned away with a sense of relief. He left the pavilion and continued along the path following the bank of a now placid stream until he came to a high brick wall on his right, ivy-covered, with a tall gate of slatted wood. Through the slats he could see into a well-kept garden with flowering shrubs and grassy paths.

It took him a moment to realize that he was at the back of Quarry House, the pink-and-white dolls' house he had noticed on his way down the lane. He was peering through the gate when a sun-hat emerged from the shrubbery and, beneath it, a woman with a secateurs in her hand.

Wycliffe said, "Good morning."

Hesitation. "Are you a policeman?" She was lean and freckled with reddish hair and, despite the floppy sun-hat, she wore trousers and a mannish jersey. Her manner was abrasive—at least suspicious. Males are unpredictable creatures. Handle with care.

Wycliffe introduced himself.

She mellowed at once. "Dear me! I had no idea that horrid little man would cause such a stir!" She opened the gate to let him in and, peeling off a gardening glove, held out a thin, aristocratic hand. "I'm Rose Gould and I live here with my twin sister, Veronica."

Since daddy died, Wycliffe thought. He said, "Obviously you know that your neighbour was killed last night; I wonder if either you or your sister heard the shot?"

She went to the back door, which stood open, and called, "Veronica! Will you come here, please?" Then she turned back to Wycliffe with a shy smile. "My sister is much better at talking to people than I. More practical."

The woman who came out of the house was a carbon copy of Rose except that she was not wearing a sun hat. Rose prattled: "The likeness is remarkable, isn't it? But you can tell us apart because Vee has an old scar just above her right eye."

"Which you put there." Veronica had a deeper voice as well as a scar.

"Yes, I know, dear, but not deliberately." Rose blushed, the colour flooding up over her freckles. "The superintendent was asking about the shot we heard last night."

"We don't know that it was a shot; it could have been anything— all we heard was a sharp crack."

"What time was this?"

Veronica said, "When we were going to bed—between a quarter to eleven and eleven o'clock."

"Did you notice anything else yesterday evening? Anyone going up or down the lane, for example?"

"Did we, dear?" Rose looked at Veronica.

Veronica shook her head. "No, I don't think so. I do remember seeing Newcombe on his way to the public house but there was certainly nothing unusual in that."

"Why didn't you like him?"

"Did we not?" Veronica was on her dignity.

"Your sister spoke of him as 'a horrid little man.' "

"Oh, did she! Well, he was. As long as his mother lived she kept control of him; he was reasonably dressed, clean and polite. Though I never liked the man I can't say that he ever gave us cause for complaint."

"And since?"

Rose was unable to resist cutting in. "Since, he's behaved abominably. Whenever he passes here, if one of us happens to be in the front garden, he laughs."

"Laughs?"

"Well, he sneers and calls out in a most unpleasant way. I try not to be out there when he passes. In fact, if it had been left to me, I should have spoken to Constable Miller about him long ago."

Veronica was contemptuous. "I don't need Miller to put Newcombe in his place!"

Wycliffe said, "The path from his cottage to the waterfall doesn't seem to be much used."

Veronica frowned. "It shouldn't be used at all; in fact, it shouldn't be there. Newcombe used to treat the woods as though they were his—setting snares and traps—until the family put a stop to it."

"The family?"

"The Beales."

"What about the path I came by from the waterfall here—I suppose that leads on to the house?"

He was aware of a sudden slight tension in Veronica's manner; she said in an offhand way, "Oh, that's quite different; it's a perfectly legitimate path—private, of course."

"But where does it go?"

"As you say—to the house." Brusque.

One of the odd features of police work: one never knows when some innocent probe will touch an exposed nerve and, if it does, whether it has anything to do with the case.

He changed the subject. "I know the Beales live at Ashill but how many of them are there? Who exactly lives there?" He asked the question in a relaxed, conversational way.

Rose said, "Oh, there are—"

Veronica cut in, "They're a very united family. Of course, the fact that they are Roman Catholic helps but it's still quite remarkable to find a family staying together as they have in these days. . . . There's Mr. Simon, the head of the family; he's a widower; his two sons, one of whom is married and lives there with his wife. Then there is his daughter—Mrs. Vicary—she lives there with her husband and *their* daughter, Esther." She broke off with a little laugh. "Have I forgotten any of them?"

Rose said, "Edward—"

"Oh, yes—Edward. He is Mr. Simon's nephew by marriage; he's a young man now but he's been there since he was a child—he was orphaned, I think."

Wycliffe said, "Quite a family! And, as you say, unusual in these days with them all continuing to live under one roof."

He thanked the sisters and told them he would send someone to take their statements about the probable time of the shot.

It was absurd for a chief super to be on the ground touting for evidence; his men would visit every house in the village and in neighbouring villages if necessary. With their clip-boards and ball-points they would gather a great mass of mostly useless information which would be typed, photocopied and filed. Eventually he would be presented with a lovely fat file of his own which he could turn over in the privacy of his office or anywhere else he fancied. But he disliked pre-packed, sterilized information almost as much as he disliked pre-packed, sterilized food. It had no taste.

Rose let him out by the garden gate, the way he had come. He continued through the trees, crossed the lawn, walked round the house and out through the tall iron gates without being challenged; as far as he knew, without being seen.

So it was possible that the killer had left Newcombe's cottage by way of the hedge and the footpath through the wood, but why would he want to?

A police incident van had arrived and was parked not far from the gates of Ashill, opposite the church. It would serve as a communication centre and as a base for his men working on the case. The duty officer was D.C. Potter—the squad's fat boy, known to intimates as The Pot. Potter was settling in, getting organized. On the table there was a duty book and a number of neatly labelled files; on the wall, a two-and-a-half-inch ordnance map of Washford and district.

Wycliffe looked upon it all with a critical eye and was satisfied.

"Have you had your lunch, Potter?"

"Over at the pub, sir."

"Any good?"

"I had a chicken curry—very nice, sir, and the beer's good."

The pub was a "free house" and not tarted up; no bar stools, no rustic tables, no phoney wrought-iron sconces, horse-brasses or flintlock pistols; only benches and tables cut in the local sawmill a century ago and polished by generations of backsides and forearms. The room was L-shaped and the smaller leg was separated from the rest by a low rail with a gate and a notice: "For customers taking meals."

It was almost two and the few local workers who had been in for a quick drink had gone again leaving only Wycliffe and two old men who were dressed alike in black jackets and caps and grey, baggy trousers. They seemed content to sit, staring into space, exchanging only occasional laconic remarks. Too late for the main dish, Wycliffe ordered a meat pie and a pint.

Harry Blatchford, the landlord, must have been over seventy himself; a large man with a high colour, bald except for a halo of tight grey curls. He had the local brogue but spoke more correctly than most of his customers for he had been a sales-rep for a firm of agricultural merchants before taking over the inn from his parents. A fat, pleasant-faced young woman with a mop of brown hair was busy washing glasses.

"There's nothing much I can tell you, Superintendent. Last night was the same as any other. Bunny sat there in his corner from about seven on; he had his usual, then about half-ten, he left. Same as always."

"But last night somebody was waiting for him at his cottage, with a gun."

"So they tell me, though it beats me why anybody would want to shoot Bunny. They tell me it was a hand-gun?"

"An automatic pistol."

Blatchford spread his great hands in a gesture of incomprehension. "As I say, it beats me."

"Perhaps you would have been a good deal less surprised if it had been a shotgun?"

Wycliffe received a cunning look. "I didn't say that, sir; you mustn't put words into my mouth."

"I gather he wasn't popular with some of the women in the village."

"Ah! I wouldn't know about that, sir; we don't have much woman talk in here, do we, Dora?"

The fat girl said, "I couldn't tell you; I never have time to listen."

Wycliffe was eating his pie at a little table near the bar. He took time to finish it off and sipped his beer.

"You've known Newcombe a long time?"

"All his life. I've always lived here; this pub belonged to my father and his father before him—way back. Of course I knew Bunny's father and mother. His father died youngish—a heart attack when he was out giving a hand in the hayfield one evening. It was the year myxo was so bad with dead and dying rabbits everywhere. Bunny's mother died only this last Christmas—a stroke—popped off just like that. She was a Truscott from Buckfast way—Emily Truscott." Blatchford chuckled. "Emily was a strong-minded woman and no mistake! She kept her son on the straight and narrow. I've heard him say in this bar that the old lady would smack his face when he stepped out of line almost up to the day she died."

"Did he wash then?"

"Had to! She was quite capable of standing him up in the yard starkers and throwing buckets of water over him. And he had to do a day's work. He'd come in here of an evening for a pint but he'd sup up and go. Emily wouldn't have him spending his time and money in here drinking."

One of the old men who had seemed not to be listening said, "Bunny liked the women. I mind there were that there maid over to Shipley—"

Blatchford cut him short. "God, Tom! You're going back a bit; he couldn't've been more than eighteen or nineteen then."

Wycliffe said, "I gather he's got an aunt in the village."

The landlord folded his huge arms on the counter. "That's right, sir. Martha Fretwell; she's his father's sister—married to Jim Fretwell, our undertaker. They live up the top of North Street. I reckon Martha had a soft spot for her nephew; he used to drop in there pretty often."

Wycliffe drained his glass and prepared to leave. "Newcombe had money to spend, apparently, but he doesn't seem to have earned much lately. Do you think—"

Blatchford laughed. "You've been listening to tales about Emily's old stocking. She might've left him a few pounds but nothing to write home about. If the old lady had money I don't know where she got it; Bunny's father was a gardener for the Beales and he did a bit of rabbiting on the side; Emily worked at Ashill, too. She was a maid there before she married and afterwards she worked there part time all the way through up to a couple of years before she died."

Wycliffe said, "What's that to do with her having or not having money?"

A broad grin. "Just that nobody ever made anything working for the Beales. There's a saying in the village—'They wouldn' give 'ee the skin of a rotten tatie.' "

Wycliffe thanked him. "I expect I'll be back."

"I reckon you will, sir."

At the door Wycliffe stopped to read an advertisement stuck to the wall, a poster in an antique format announcing Washford Horse and Hiring Fair, to be held on May Day—the following Friday.

The landlord said, "Have you ever been to our fair, sir?"

"Never."

"You don't know what you've missed. Takes you back; a touch of the old nostalgia."

He made it sound like rheumatism.

Chapter Two

The village drowsed in afternoon sunshine; in school, children were singing "Bobby Shafto." Wycliffe strolled up the main street in the leisurely fashion of a tourist. On one side a moorland stream slid by in its cobbled channel, bridged outside each front door by a single slab of granite. On the other side of the street, interspersed with the houses, were three or four shops: Samuel Brimblecombe, Tobacconist and Confectioner; Finucane's General Store and Post Office; and a depressing little shop with tins of paint, rolls of faded wallpaper, and a few plastic bowls and buckets in the window—Chas. Alford, Household and Domestic. Farther up the hill there was a Methodist chapel with an impressive granite façade and another substantial building labelled simply, "The Institute."

The windows of the houses had their curtains almost drawn; no sign of life from any of them, though Wycliffe had a feeling that his every movement was observed. He felt a bit like the Lone Ranger entering town, the only one who doesn't know that Billy the Kid is holding up the bank.

At the top of the street the houses gave way to fields which, at no great distance, surrendered to the open moor and finally to the twin tors which, though they were not very high, dominated the horizon.

A discreet board; gold letters on a black ground: Jas. Fretwell, Builder and Undertaker; a double-fronted house, windows and door painted a gleaming black, the panes of glass shining and the curtains almost meeting. Wycliffe decided to call on Martha Fretwell. She was a dumpy little woman, grey-haired with a pink-and-white complexion any girl might have envied.

Wycliffe learned Bunny's first name from her: "You've come about our Morley. P.C. Miller was here this morning to tell me. I couldn't believe my ears! Who could be wicked enough to do such a thing? I mean he's been a foolish boy but he never did anybody any real harm. . . ." Her voice was rich and smooth as butter. Although her blue eyes misted over she could not subdue her natural cheerfulness for long. "Come in, do!"

In the little sitting-room the polished furniture, the framed photographs, the embroidered satin cushions and plastic flowers seemed to be waiting, as a stage-set waits for the actors. Incongruously, there was a roll-top desk against one wall, for this was where the bereaved came to "make arrangements."

She put Wycliffe to sit in one of the uncut-moquette armchairs and sat herself on the edge of the other, smoothing the wrinkles from her skirt.

"O' course, I can't deny I been worried about him; he let himself go since Emily died, something terrible. . . ." She screwed up her little mouth and lowered her voice. "He didn't keep himself clean and he took to drinking more than was good for him and more than he could afford. I blame Emily; she ruled the poor fellow with a rod of iron when she was alive and when she went he just didn't know how to cope. . . . As I say, I was worried, but I never expected anything like this! My dear life—no!"

"Did he come to see you often?"

"Two or three times a week—he always did, from the time he was a little lad. Then it was my home-made toffee, and I suppose he got into the habit. Lately he's been coming in the morning when I'm about my work but it didn't matter because he was no trouble. He'd just sit there in the kitchen; I'd make him a cup of tea and he'd stay for a quarter of an hour or so. Then, all of a sudden, he'd get up and say, 'Well, I must be off, Auntie!' And he'd go."

"Did he have much to say?"

"No, Morley was no talker, but he'd listen to me rattling on and just put in the odd word now and then." She smiled and clasped her plump, ringed fingers in her lap.

Outside in the street the sun was shining but in this little parlour with the curtains almost meeting it was difficult to see the pictures on the walls.

"Did you visit his mother when she was alive?"

"Never!" Pursed lips. "And Emily never set foot inside my house neither."

"Have you noticed any change in him lately?"

"Change? What sort of change would you be meaning?" She did not wait for an answer but went on, "I don't know, I'm sure! All I can think of is that he asked me some funny questions I couldn't make head or tail of."

"What sort of questions?"

"Well, one day he asked me if I had a birth certificate." She laughed girlishly. "Well, I told him I had and he wanted to know where I got it. I said Mother must've got it when I was born and she gave it to me when I got married.

"Then he wanted to know if somebody didn't have a birth certificate, could they get one, and I told him all you had to do was to go the register office in Newton and pay them to make one out. He didn't say any more about it that day but two or three days later he wanted to know if you could get somebody else's certificate. My dear life! I was more flummoxed than ever to think what he could be after. . . . I told him I didn't know but that I would ask Jim—that's my husband. He said not to do that, it didn't matter."

"Was there any difficulty over his mother's will?"

Martha laughed. "Will? I ask you! What would Emily be doing, making a will? She had nothing to leave but that tumbled-down old cottage and a few sticks of furniture. And who would she leave it to but Morley anyway?"

"No money?"

She screwed up her lips, pouting. "A few pounds maybe, I'd say there most likely was, and that's what Morley's been spending on drink these past few months—but not what you'd call *money.*"

A timber lorry grinding its way up the street in low gear shattered the peace of the whole village. Wycliffe waited until the unseemly racket had subsided.

"Morley's mother worked for the Beales, didn't she?"

For some reason Martha frowned before answering. "She did; she went into service at Ashill when she was no more than fourteen and she worked there, living in, until she married my brother, Tom. Tom was their gardener. When Morley was born Emily went back there part time and she was at their beck and call one way and another till a year or two before she died. Emily thought the sun rose and set on 'the family' as she called them. You'd hardly believe, but she wanted to become a Catholic and have Morley brought up Catholic, but Tom put his foot down; he was born and reared a Wesleyan like all of us and he wasn't having none of that old nonsense!"

Neither the Beales nor Emily rated highly in Martha's charts.

Wycliffe was cautious. "Your nephew's interest in birth certificates . . . you don't think he could have had doubts about his own parentage?"

An old-fashioned look and a pause to consider how much could or should be said to this pleasant-mannered policeman who looked more like a vicar. "I don't know, and that's the truth." Then she added in a burst of frankness, "I don't know neither whether he had reason. All I can say is mother and father thought our Tom should've had more sense than to marry Emily. As a girl, she was no better than she ought to be." She smoothed the arm of her chair with the flat of her hand. "And I don't mind telling you, because nowadays people don't think twice about such things, that it was all fixed up in a hurry because Emily was expecting."

Wycliffe said casually, "Simon Beale must have been a young man at that time."

A shrewd look. "In his late twenties. Of course his father was alive then; a real martinet he was. He wouldn't stand for no what you might call nonsense."

"Did Simon have any brothers?"

Her expression did not change. "No brothers, but two sisters—older than he was and both dead and gone now."

She came to the door with him and watched as he walked back down the street towards the police caravan by the church.

Three or four women were gossiping with a little red-headed man in a grey overall who stood in the doorway of the shop which sold wallpaper, Chas. Alford, Household and Domestic. They stopped talking as he went by and watched him openly, their attitudes neither friendly nor hostile. He had a feeling that the village was engaged in making up its mind about Bunny Newcombe's death and, when it had, what was said would follow the party line.

Martha Fretwell was shrewd and she had been careful not to contest the notion that Simon Beale might have got Emily pregnant. She was not averse to discrediting the Beales and Emily, even if it made a cuckold of her own brother. To Martha, and probably to the rest of the village, facts were less important than what they wanted to believe.

All the same, Simon was about the right age. But could Bunny have been fool enough to think that even if he was Simon's bastard the fact would appear on his birth certificate? In any case, was it likely that after nearly half a century Simon would settle the affair with a gun?

Kersey was waiting for him in the incident van and they sat in the little interview room, a cubicle two yards square, with a notice on the wall defining the rights of citizens under police interrogation.

Kersey, in the early stages of yet another attempt to kick the smoking habit, felt in his pocket and withdrew his hand with a lost look. He said, "Smith checked the register for nine-millimetre automatics and there's only one in the subdivision. Property of Nicholas Beale—Simon's eldest, ex-army—a captain. The gun is a Beretta M951, the type issued as a sidearm to the Italian army in the middle fifties. It seems Beale picked it up while serving in Cyprus."

"It's been sent for tests?"

"No, that's the point. As a matter of fact I went along to Ashill myself out of curiosity. Nicholas was out and I spoke to Simon first, but Nicky turned up while I was there. He wasn't exactly matey but he made no bones about showing me where he kept the gun—a cupboard in his study—but it wasn't there. Nicked, according to him."

"A break-in?"

"Could be. Certainly the lock of the cupboard had been forced."

"And the first Beale knew of it was when you asked to see the gun?"

"So he says. I think you should see for yourself, sir. To me it's got a smell."

"Anything other than the gun missing?"

"About twenty rounds, his service medals, and a few other souvenirs of the army."

"What sort of chap is he?"

Kersey scratched his stubbly chin. "Forty-five or -six, a bachelor; stiff as a frozen haddock and about as chatty. He's hooked on the Peninsular War and spends his time re-fighting the battles with maps and what-not. The villagers call him 'the General' and old Simon, who's used to lording it over people, is wary of Nicky. As a matter of fact, before he turned up I had the impression that Simon was trying to warn me of, or off, him. I wondered why."

"Does Nicholas have anything to do with the business?"

"Seems not. Brother Maurice is managing director and the old man's son-in-law, Frank Vicary, is secretary-accountant or something. Vicary started as a clerk in the office but married Gertrude, Simon's only daughter; now he's the kingpin of the show. Esther— the girl you met—is their daughter and they all live in Ashill with the rest of the clan. One big happy family, though that wasn't the impression I got."

Kersey himself looked anything but happy, but this was due to continuing self-denial.

He went on: "Incidentally, Maurice's wife looks a bit like an ageing pro. Out of her element, I fancy. There's also a young man called Edward. I'm not sure where he fits in but he's a painter— canvas, not walls."

Wycliffe said, "You must be picking up a fair amount of gossip from the house-to-house reports—what about Simon, any wild oats?"

Kersey's rubbery face wrinkled into a broad grin. "Well, he's seventy-four, so by this time I should think they'd sprouted or gone mouldy or whatever wild oats do. There's some gossip about him when he was younger but nothing specific."

"A week or two before he died Newcombe was showing an interest in birth certificates."

"Whose?"

"He didn't say; his questions to his aunt were general but he brought up the subject more than once. She didn't discount the notion that he might be Simon's by-blow; his mother was a servant at Ashill and she, very conveniently, married the gardener."

"What would he expect to find out from a birth certificate?"

"I don't know, but I gather he wasn't one of the world's brightest."

Kersey frowned. "Would anybody care now? Unless, of course, Newcombe was trying to get money out of the old man. If so, he waited long enough."

"He may not have known until after his mother died or she might have stopped him from using what he did know."

Kersey nodded. "That's a line, sir, certainly. Anyway, the Beales are worth getting to know, if only for the experience."

Five or six steps took them to the wrought-iron gates of Ashill, which were well preserved, as was the ironwork balcony which ran the length of the first floor (with partitions at intervals to make promiscuity more difficult or more adventurous). The house had round-headed windows and the front was stucco with a moulded cornice—very civilized and refined Regency. The doorbell was answered by a little old woman with a face as brown and wrinkled as a peach-stone, and a waspish manner.

"Police again! You'll have to come in, I suppose, and I'll tell 'em you're here."

In the hall she hesitated whether to leave them standing or take them into the drawing-room; she decided on the drawing-room. "In here, then."

Kersey muttered, "I was left in the hall."

Wycliffe spoke to the old woman, "You must have been here in Emily Newcombe's time."

He received a baleful glance from her little dark eyes. "That's as may be but I don't know anything about that son of hers if that's what you're after." She shuffled off in her carpet slippers.

The room was dimly lit and sombre; heavy Victorian furniture upholstered in red plush, a grand piano covered with a fringed cloth, overvarnished oil-paintings of Dartmoor in heavy, gilded frames. Above the mantelpiece there was a full-length portrait of a distinguished-looking old gentleman wearing a high collar, a cutaway jacket and tight trousers. Surely Simon's grandfather, the founder of the firm. In his picture, he looked like a tenth earl but in his younger days he must have known what it was to stand under an arcade of buckets and brooms being obsequious to the right people.

The house was silent as a church; not a footstep, not a cough. Kersey whispered, "It's like a morgue where they aren't quite dead."

Simon came silently into the room, tall and frail-looking, silvery-haired. He held out a thin hand, cold as a fish. "Ah, Mr. Wycliffe; I suppose you've come about this Newcombe business."

Wycliffe was cool. "I've come to talk to your son about a missing gun, registered in his name."

The white eyebrows went up. "Really? I thought your inspector had dealt with that earlier. However, if it's Nicholas you want to see, you had better come with me."

They followed the old man along an L-shaped passage to the other side of the house. The interior of Ashill belied the cheerful Regency front it presented to the world: heavy, red carpeting, brown woodwork and bottle-green walls. They were taken to a long room with french windows which could be opened onto the garden but were now closed. Even so it was an oasis of sunlight in the gloomy house though the room itself was shabby and threadbare. A couple of armchairs, a sofa, a desk, and bookshelves with the regimented spines of unused books.

Most of the space was taken up with trestle-tables on which the battlefields of the Peninsular War had been reconstructed in a combination of relief maps and coloured blocks and flags to represent fighting units. Vimiero, Rolica, Talavera . . . on to Fuentes, Vitoria and Toulouse, the names of the battles and of the generals involved were repeated on box files stacked on improvised shelves.

Simon said, in a plaintive voice, "This used to be the library, now my son uses it for his . . . for his work."

Nicholas was seated at the desk with maps and charts spread out before him. He got up from his chair; tall, sallow-skinned with very dark hair, he had a black moustache so meticulously trimmed that it looked false. Though thin, like his father, Nicholas had a low paunch so that, in profile, he was rather like General de Gaulle. He scarcely acknowledged Simon's introduction and did not invite them to sit down. Father and son stood facing each other for a while as though engaged in some private contest of wills, then Nicholas said, "I suppose you want to know about my gun; I kept it in that cupboard."

He pointed to one of two cupboards by the fireplace. "You will see that the lock has been forced."

It was true, the woodwork around the lock was bruised though not splintered; the damage was not conspicuous and it was evident that very little effort had been needed to force the flimsy lock.

"When did you first realize that the cupboard had been broken open?"

"When your officer came earlier and asked to see the gun." Nicholas ignored the fact that Kersey, the officer concerned, was standing within a yard of him.

"Was anything else taken?"

"Apart from the gun and ammunition, my service medals and other souvenirs of army life."

Nicholas moved with deliberation and his speech was precise. Wycliffe had the impression of an automaton who would go through its prescribed routine without regard to those about him. When Nicholas looked in his direction the brown eyes seemed to focus on some point beyond his head.

"When did you last see the gun?"

"I can't remember. Possibly about three weeks ago when I went to the cupboard for some papers I kept there."

"Have you at any time seen signs of a forced entry—perhaps through the french windows, or of an intruder having been in this room?"

Simon intervened with a certain animation, "That is exactly what I've been saying to my son. Someone came in through those windows when they had been left open. It would be quite easy—"

Nicholas answered Wycliffe's question, cutting across his father's words, "I have never noticed any signs of an intruder."

"Are the windows often left open?"

"Sometimes, when the weather is hot."

"Even when there is no one in the room?"

Nicholas shrugged his shoulders but did not answer.

Wycliffe persisted, "Do you think it likely that someone came in from the garden when the windows were open, broke open your cupboard and took the gun?"

"The gun is gone."

"Did many people know that you had a gun and where you kept it?"

"It was not a secret."

The man seemed remote, indifferent. Surely he must realize the significance of the missing gun?

Wycliffe said, "There are two cupboards, both locked, and, looking round, I see a number of drawers, yet it seems the thief went straight to the cupboard where the gun was, and only to that cupboard—is that so?"

"Apparently."

Wycliffe went to the french windows and put his hand on the lever which operated the opening mechanism. "May I?"

Beale neither acceded nor refused but merely watched. The catch yielded after an effort and the window ground open reluctantly on rusty hinges. Wycliffe closed it again.

"Have you any idea who might have taken your gun, Captain Beale?"

"None."

"You realize that we shall have to inquire among members of your family?"

No reply.

Did he actually want to embarrass his father and involve the whole household?

Simon said, "I think you are drawing an unwarrantable conclusion, Mr. Wycliffe."

Wycliffe turned on him the bland, blank stare which most people found disconcerting, and said, "I haven't drawn any conclusion, I am making inquiries." He turned to Nicholas. "Isn't a Beretta an unusual gun for a British officer?"

"The Beretta was not my service pistol; I carried a Browning like everybody else; the Beretta was a gift from a Greek Cypriot who insisted that I had done him a service."

It was obvious that no more would be got from Nicholas.

Wycliffe said, "Mr. Kersey will arrange for statements to be taken from you and other members of the household."

It was Simon who saw them out; they left Nicholas standing by his desk, stroking his moustache, apparently unmoved.

Retired district nurse Ruby Price lived alone on the northern fringe of the village, on the very edge of the moor. Her little house had been built before the First World War by an eccentric Oxford don as a summer retreat. It had three rooms on the ground floor and one above—perched on the rest like a squat tower to command the countryside. Ruby was seventy-five but she had worn well, her hair retained glints of the original gold, she had a healthy tan, her smooth complexion was free of blemishes, and her lean angular body was that of a still active woman. At a quarter to four Ruby was in her upstair room, sitting in an old wicker chair by the window which looked towards the moor. There was another window in the opposite wall, facing south over the village, so that the room got the sun as well as a moorland view.

On a table at her side was a tray set for afternoon tea; matching china in a floral design, *petits fours* and oolong tea; intimations of gentility. A marmalade cat slept on a cushion at her feet while she listened to a play on the radio. She was hard of hearing and the volume was turned up so that disembodied voices vibrated through the speaker.

Since her arrival there at the age of twenty-four, Ruby had made Washford her own; she had first rented, then bought the little house in which she still lived and after thirty-six years delivering babies, administering enemas, dressing ulcerated legs and rubbing aged, bedridden backs, there was scarcely a door in the village or in neighbouring hamlets at which she went through the formality of knocking. Since her retirement she had assumed the role of maiden aunt to the whole community; she visited the people in their homes, encouraged them to tell her their troubles and confide their secrets, never doubting her welcome. She received few overt snubs, though by some she was regarded as an interfering busybody.

But Ruby was content with herself and, broadly, with her life, though she dreaded the prospect of being forced eventually to endure the unendurable, the brisk professional caring and the ineffable companionship of an old-people's home.

She reached for a pair of binoculars which had belonged to her sea-captain father, raised them to her eyes and swept the moor: a foreground of tiny stone-walled fields, unchanged since they were plotted by Iron Age Celts; then a rougher terrain of heather and bog, away to the twin tors—one rising smooth and contoured like a woman's breast, the other topped with a rugged castle of Brobding-nagian boulders. Ruby focused on Druid's Rock—a pinnacle of gran-ite about two miles off. Earlier she had seen Edward sketching near the rock but now ponies grazed there. On his way home Edward would call to see her as he always did when he had been out on the moor; a timid, warm-hearted boy, now her only contact with the family—or almost. . . . Never mind! They would need her before she needed them.

Edward had given her one of his paintings—a view of the moor in winter from this very window; it hung on the wall above her collec-tion of snapshots of the babies she had brought into the world. With a sigh Ruby put down her binoculars and poured herself an-other cup of tea, then she closed her eyes. The play was reaching its climax and she settled to listen with greater attention. At that mo-ment she became conscious of a movement close at hand; she opened her eyes again—startled, and in that instant her world was shattered in a single blinding flash.

Instead of going back to the police van, Wycliffe walked in the churchyard—still a good place to get the feel of a village—and here all was as it should have been. The Blatchfords, the Fretwells, the Endacotts, Newcombes and Finucanes were all recorded in moss-covered stone and slate, the credentials of the village.

The church itself, built while Henry Tudor was still trying out his Welsh bottom on the English throne—was undecorated Perpendic-ular, no nonsense. The church was dedicated to St. Dorothea, the martyred young lady who had, posthumously, sent her judge a bas-ket of fruit and flowers from the Elysian Fields. To prove it, there was the basket, carved in stone, above the south porch.

No Beales in the churchyard, no memorial tablets to the family in the church; then he remembered they were Catholics, but the origi-nal squires—the Drews—were commemorated through several gen-erations, in stone and brass.

He came out again into the sunshine, thinking of the missing pistol—of the possibilities. Someone who knew about the gun—not family—prowling about the grounds when the french windows were open, had nipped in, picked the right cupboard, opened it and made off with the gun, the ammunition and Nicholas's souvenirs.

Alternatively the intruder, not knowing about the gun, had come upon it by chance while looking for anything worth taking; then presumably he had said, "Oh goody! Now I can shoot that bastard Newcombe!" Or words to that effect.

Wycliffe growled like a disgruntled bear. The fact was that everything pointed to an inside job—one of the family. But would any of them be stupid enough not to realize that the family would be prime suspects?

And if it was a family affair, a crime arising out of repressed hatreds and jealousies within the Beale household, it was hard to see why an illiterate recluse, living in squalor on the edge of the estate, should be its victim. The victim—that was his starting point. What could Newcombe have had or done or known which made it necessary or worthwhile to kill him?

There was his interest in birth certificates. Generally such documents tell only what people allow to be known, but for some innocents any bit of printed paper carries the seal of ultimate truth.

A young man was coming down the path which cut through the churchyard from the direction of the moor. Slim and dark and pale, with large doe-like eyes, as he drew nearer he moved off the path on to the grass to avoid a possible encounter. He carried, slung over his shoulder, a complicated pack which included a folding easel. After he had passed Wycliffe was aware of his nervous backward glance and turned to watch him. He passed through the lich-gate, crossed the Green and entered through the gates of Ashill.

The young painter Kersey had mentioned. Was he a Beale? Wycliffe had his answer sooner than he expected.

"Good afternoon, Mr. Wycliffe."

He faced round abruptly. One of the Gould twins—no scar, so Rose.

"That was Edward Beale, our local painter; Simon Beale's nephew by marriage. He was orphaned as a young child and Simon adopted him. They say he will make a name for himself in the art world."

Rose was wearing a floral dress in shades of mauve with a head-scarf to match and she had a little spaniel dog on a lead.

"I was taking Jasper for his walk when I saw you. . . . I must confess I hoped that we might meet. . . . We were speaking of the Beales—such an interesting family I always think. So much enter-prise. . . ."

Wycliffe smiled. "I think there is something you want to tell me."

She coloured like a schoolgirl. "It's a small thing and my sister feels very strongly that we should not involve ourselves. . . ." She smiled up at him, inviting understanding.

"I'm sure that it is a coincidence but the police are always asking people to cooperate. . . . It was yesterday—Sunday afternoon, at about this time, and I was taking Jasper for his walk, but yesterday we went *down* the lane, towards the Newton road and, of course, we had to pass Newcombe's cottage, both going and coming back. We don't go that way very often, do we Jasper? But we do it sometimes out of *bravado!*" She looked away in embarrassment at the admis-sion. "It was on our way back, when we were a few yards from the cottage, I heard men's voices. I could not distinguish the words at first but as I drew level with the gate I heard a man say in a fairly aggressive manner, 'You've done very well out of this, Newcombe!' "

"Did you see who it was speaking?"

She nodded. "Yes, I did. It was Mr. Vicary, Simon Beale's son-in-law—such a strange-looking man. . . . He reminds me of those monkeys with wrinkled faces who look like little old men. . . . At any rate it was Mr. Vicary, and he was talking to Newcombe."

"Did they see you?"

"No, I don't think so. We were very quiet, weren't we, Jasper?"

"Did you hear anything else?"

She coloured. "Well, I wasn't exactly listening, Superintendent . . . I wouldn't like you to think. . . . But Mr. Vicary's voice *was* raised. When Newcombe spoke it was in his usual rather horrid wheedling tone, like Uriah Heep I always say, and I didn't hear what he said but Mr. Vicary's words were quite clear. He said, 'If you adopt that attitude, Newcombe, you are making the biggest mistake of your life!' " She was looking up at him, half nervous, half excited. "I don't suppose it's of any importance but you did say . . . In any case, I do hope that you won't find it necessary to mention what I've told you to Veronica. She has a very high regard for 'the family' as she calls them."

Wycliffe thanked her and stooped to speak to Jasper, who looked up at him with large, bored brown eyes.

It was odd to reflect that the Misses Gould existed in the same world as the muggers, rioters and terrorists who made headlines every day. Jane Austen Rules! OK?

Wycliffe returned to the police van and to Kersey. "I don't suppose you know the superintendent registrar in Newton?"

"As it happens, I've met him: he's a dry old stick called Endacott; looks like a Dickensian lawyer; probably still writes out his certificates with a goose quill."

"Ring him up and ask if he's had a visit from Newcombe recently —or any enquiries concerning the Beale family."

Kersey put through the call and spoke to a furry, female voice which said, spitefully pleased, "We closed for public business at five. If you have any enquiry you should telephone or call after ten o'clock in the morning."

Kersey grinned. "Put down your knitting, love, and concentrate. I'm a police officer and I want to speak to Mr. Endacott."

Silence, so that Kersey thought she had hung up on him, but quite suddenly there was a bark from the receiver: "Mr. Endacott here, what is it you want?"

"Detective Inspector Kersey (it rolled nicely off his tongue though still a bit unfamiliar)—I want to know if you've had an enquiry recently from a Mr. Newcombe—Morley Newcombe—a little fat man who probably looked and smelt like a tramp."

"Any member of the public who pays the appropriate fee—"

"Yes, I know all about that, Mr. Endacott, but we are anxious to know about this particular member of the public who happens to have got himself shot."

The official mind churned almost audibly. "In that case I suppose I am justified in telling you that a man answering your description did call at the office; I dealt with him myself."

"When?"

"Last week sometime—I remember, it was market day, so it must have been Wednesday—Wednesday afternoon."

"What did he want?"

"He wanted to see the entry in the register relating to his birth."

"Anything else?"

"He requested two other searches and had sight of those entries also."

"What were they?"

Mr. Endacott sighed, "I suppose I am in order in telling you all this! If you will hold on a moment . . ."

He was back in a couple of minutes. "The first entry concerned the marriage of Francis Vicary to Gertrude Rosemary Beale, and the second recorded the birth of their child, Esther."

"Did he ask for certified copies of any of the entries?"

"No."

"Did he seem satisfied with the information you were able to give him?"

A dry cackle like tearing paper: "We are not in the business of customer satisfaction, Inspector; we merely make our records available to those entitled to see them."

"I think you know what I mean. Did he seem surprised or disappointed by the facts as recorded?"

Hesitation. "I must admit that he seemed disappointed and inclined to blame me for it. He muttered something about having wasted his time—not that I would have supposed that to have much value."

Kersey thanked the old boy and said that he would send an officer —with the necessary fees—to obtain certified copies of the entries which had interested Newcombe. Then he looked at Wycliffe, "What do you make of that, sir?"

Wycliffe shook his head. Whichever way they turned they came up against Beales. Means, Opportunity and Motive—the cardinal heads under which suspicion must be justified. Means presented no problem; almost certainly Newcombe had been shot with Nicholas's pistol. Opportunity was equally simple; the footpath from Ashill to

Newcombe's yard guaranteed easy and private access. Motive? Well, it looked as though one might be suggesting itself.

Kersey said, "Surely the whole family can't be in cahoots?"

As often happened, he and Wycliffe were thinking along the same lines.

Simon was alone in the dining-room where the table was set for dinner with eight places. Although the Vicarys had a more or less self-contained flat on the first floor, it had become the custom for the whole family to dine together. Maurice and Frank arrived home from the firm's offices in the city at six-thirty, and dinner was at seven.

Simon poured himself a dry sherry, took it to the window and stood, looking out. A broad lawn on a gentle slope, then woodland with the ground dropping more steeply to the valley below. Through the trees to his left, not yet in full leaf, he could glimpse the icing-sugar pink and white of Quarry House.

He was badly shaken. The shooting of Newcombe, Nicky's missing gun, the superintendent's questions, interrogation of the whole household—wasn't it obvious what the police thought? He dared not put his own thoughts into words. Had there been an outsider who had come in through the french window? He had tried to lead the superintendent to think so but, in fact, the window was rarely opened and the man had seen that for himself. The alternative . . . the alternative was unthinkable. He shrugged angrily; it was as though Nicholas had deliberately set out to arouse police suspicion, yet he had more reason than— But it was dangerous to think like that.

Nicholas and Maurice: Simon felt that he had little cause to be gratified in his sons.

Someone came into the room and he turned sharply, then saw with relief that it was Frank and not one of the others. Childish! But he had come to depend on his son-in-law, and not only in business matters.

Vicary went to the sideboard and poured himself a whisky. He was a little man, dark, with something oddly simian about him; his face was lined and he had small, deeply set eyes, restless and probing. It was strange that there should be such a rapport between two such different men.

Vicary said, "You've had a bad day."

They had twice discussed the Newcombe affair on the telephone; now Simon threw up his hands in a half-humorous gesture of despair.

Vicary brought his drink over to the window and the two men stood, side by side. "What finally happened about Nicky's gun?"

Simon told him of the second police visit and Vicary listened without interrupting, then he said, "I shouldn't worry too much; the police have to be seen to be doing something. Look at it this way: would anybody in this house be silly enough to draw suspicion on themselves by using a gun, kept in the house, and known to the police?"

But Simon was not reassured. "You may be right, Frank—I hope you are, but I've a feeling . . ." He made a vague gesture with his hands. "A feeling that Newcombe isn't the real target."

Vicary said in a dry voice, "It's Newcombe who is dead."

Simon sighed. "I know . . . I know. I'm probably talking nonsense but I wish you hadn't gone to see him on Sunday afternoon. If the police find out you were there and the reason—"

"They won't find out. How can they? And even if they did the business of the pension is a perfectly reasonable explanation."

"Of course! I'm getting old, Frank. One gets obsessed by an idea. . . ." He broke off, then changed the subject. "Have you been up to the flat since you've been home?"

A wry smile. "You mean, have I seen Gertrude. I've just come down; she has one of her headaches and she won't be down for dinner."

The old man nodded. "I was afraid of that; I saw her earlier and it was obvious . . . I suppose it's understandable, this is bound to affect her, but I wish she would get out more—make some effort. She spends too much time up there brooding; and with Naomi—well, they've nothing in common. . . ."

Simon's nephew, Edward, came in. Edward was very thin, very dark, with large brown eyes made more conspicuous by the extreme pallor of his face. "Oh . . ." He hesitated just inside the door, his manner alert and furtive like some shy nocturnal animal caught in the light. "I'm sorry, I thought I was late for dinner. . . ." He had a streak of green paint across one cheek.

The two men ignored him. Edward looked around uncomfortably, then went to sit at the table.

Simon spoke, lowering his voice, "Have you said any more to Nicky about buying him out?"

Vicary grimaced. "As I told you, when I first mentioned it he said nothing but I had the impression he was prepared to think it over. Last night I brought up the subject again and he just went over the top. You know that kind of cold fury—it really took my breath away, it was so unexpected."

"What did he say?"

Vicary shrugged. "What didn't he say!" He lowered his voice still further, glancing across at Edward. "First that I had insulted him; second, that I was an interloper, doing my best to take over the firm and the family with it; third, that I had ruined Gertrude's life and that I was turning her into an alcoholic. . . ." Vicary smiled a wry smile. "There was more; none of it pleasant."

Simon sighed. "I'm sorry; I had no idea he would take it like that or I wouldn't have suggested it. Now he's got involved with this Gould woman I thought he might be glad to realize his capital and he can't do that outside of the family."

"Well, he certainly isn't going to sell to me and I've upset him."

Simon was dismissive. "I shouldn't let it worry you. He's been the same ever since he was a child—touchy and unpredictable, liable to tantrums."

A woman's voice came from the hall, strident and minatory: "I think it was unwise of you, Esther, getting *involved*. Going down there to feed that man's animals! Of course, what you do is no business of mine, but we really don't want to get mixed up in this sordid affair! I'm sure your grandfather would agree."

They came in together; Maurice's wife—Naomi—and Esther. Esther gave no sign that she heeded her aunt, no sign that she had even heard.

Naomi was in her mid-forties; plump and running to fat, and a bottle blonde. Her cheeks sagged a little on either side of a petulant over-made-up little mouth. She switched on a cluster of lights over the dining table and the room was laid bare in all its shabby late-Victorian pretension. Naomi's fierce little eyes darted around. "Where's Maurice? Isn't he down yet? And Nicholas—surely it isn't going to be another of those nights!"

There was a move towards the table and Vicary said, "Gertrude isn't coming down."

Naomi looked at him, lips pursed. "So Esther told me. Is there any point in sending something up?"

Vicary said, "I think not."

Naomi sat at the foot of the table as Simon took his place at the head; the others arranged themselves, Esther across the table from Edward, Vicary next to Naomi. The old servant wheeled in a heated trolley which she manoeuvred into position on Naomi's right. "There's more soup if you want it." She shuffled out, her slippers dragging across the carpet. Naomi started to ladle out the soup and plates passed from hand to hand.

Maurice came in, shorter and stouter than his father and brother and, unlike them, he had a high colour. He sat down, tucking in his napkin, a greedy man. "I hope I haven't delayed you all; I had a telephone call. . . ." He spoke busily as though time pressed. "Where's Nicky? And Gertrude—isn't Gertie coming down?"

Nobody answered.

He went on: "This is a bad business! First Newcombe, now this upset over Nicky's gun. . . . Who on earth would want to kill the fellow? There must be a madman in the village; there's no other explanation, and to think he must actually have been in this house. . . . How else could he have got hold of the gun?"

Nicholas came in and took his seat without a word. He arranged his napkin, rearranged his place-setting to his satisfaction and accepted the plate of soup Naomi handed him with no more than a slight movement of the lips; but this was normal.

Simon gathered their attention and recited the grace before meals.

They began to eat and there was silence in the whole room except for sounds incidental to the meal.

Simon looked round the table. All was as it would have been on any other night. If tonight they were conscious of any added tension they gave no sign. He thought: We are like actors in a play that has run for too long with the same cast. His gaze rested on his nephew, Edward, and he saw the streak of green paint on the boy's face. Simon always thought of Edward as "the boy," though he must now be twenty-one or two. The child of his wife's much younger sister, Simon had adopted him at the age of eight, in tragic circumstances. He had done so to please his wife. But Edward had been a sickly child and an ailing youth. Now that he was a young man he and Simon were wholly estranged. Though he tried to feel compassion, Simon's attitude was one of contempt. He blamed Naomi who had had the upbringing of the boy after his wife's death. "Made him into a sissy! A milksop!"

If Esther had been a boy! But he could hardly bring himself to wish Esther other than she was. He never tired of looking at her. In his private thoughts he called her his Botticelli virgin. . . . Was she a virgin? Probably not in the technical sense; few girls of her age were, it seemed. But emotionally—no doubt there. He envied the man who would one day transform that serene countenance. . . .

Esther was watching Edward, her eyes steady and intent gave nothing away. What did the look mean? Was it contemptuous? sympathetic? protective? Simon could not guess what their relationship was but he suspected that it might be more intimate than appeared. He was sometimes disturbed by a vision of the boy's thin, pallid body writhing on the naked girl while she lay still and passive, staring at the ceiling with those concealing eyes.

Nicholas watched Esther—not openly, but with quick, shy, surreptitious glances, like an adolescent. Despite his troubles, Simon chuckled to himself. Nicky had never grown up; the business in Germany was proof of that, if proof were needed. Now he played Sir Galahad to the woman down the lane and enticed Esther into the library when he could, to lecture her on his battles.

Edward looked at nobody, he kept his eyes down and plied his spoon; but there was something wrong. Instead of those fastidious, precise movements which often irritated Simon, the boy's hand was trembling so that his soup spilled back into the plate. Suddenly he dropped his spoon with a clatter, got up from his chair, pushing it back so that it toppled over, and made for the door.

Naomi called after him in her most tragic voice: "Edward!"

What a fool the woman was! Abruptly the mixture of thoughts, fears and emotions which had been troubling Simon crystallized into anger. He shouted: "For God's sake, woman, leave him alone!"

Naomi looked as though she had been slapped.

Esther stood up. "I'll go with him."

"I'm called Gratton—Nancy Gratton—and I work for Mrs. Finucane in the shop. She said I ought to come and tell you . . ."

"About what?"

The girl had turned up at the police caravan after leaving work and was talking to Kersey.

"About Sunday night. I was down the lane by Ashill, sitting on the seat with my friend—"

"What time was this?"

"I don't know exactly but we saw Bunny Newcombe on his way home from the pub so it must've been about half-past ten."

"What happened?"

"Nothing really—he made some silly joke like always and went on down to his cottage."

Kersey thought she was really a very pretty girl—dark hair and eyes with pale clear skin, but she had never learned how to stand or sit and so she was round-shouldered. Kersey nagged his own two daughters about posture like a Victorian governess.

"How far is the seat from the cottage?"

"Not far. Maybe fifty yards or a bit less. The seat is under the trees but the cottage was in the moonlight so we could see it all right."

"You heard the shot—is that it?"

She nodded. "Not long after he went in. It was funny—not exactly a bang, more a sort of crack. It sounded as though it came from the cottage but my friend said that was daft. He said it was a poacher in the woods and that shots sounded different at night. . . ." She shifted uncomfortably in her seat, glanced at Kersey and away again. "After all, it didn't seem likely that it came from the cottage, did it?"

"So you didn't do anything about it."

She shook her head. "No, and when I heard what had happened I felt awful."

Kersey said, "No need: you couldn't have done anything for Newcombe, he was killed instantly. How long did you stay on the seat after the shot?"

"Oh, quite a while; we had a bit of a row."

"About the shot?"

"Well, it started with that but you know how things go. . . ." She smiled a worried smile.

"Could anyone have come out of the cottage into the lane without you seeing them?"

"I'm sure they couldn't have. Apart from anything else that gate makes enough row to wake the dead."

She had said her piece and Kersey was expecting her to get up and go, but Nancy sat tight, looking uncomfortable, hands gripped between her thighs. Outside a herd of brown cows lumbered past the van on their way from milking, back to pasture.

"There's something else?"

"I saw a light in the cottage *before* Bunny passed us on his way home."

"A light?"

"Like somebody using a candle or torch—moving around. From the seat you can only see the upstairs and there's only one window that faces up the lane."

"You saw the light—was that all?"

She was frowning and she hesitated before saying: "I saw a shadow—I *thought* it was a woman's shadow but I couldn't be sure."

"How long was this before you saw Newcombe?"

She shrugged. "Ten minutes? About that."

"What made you think it was a woman's shadow? Try to remember."

"I've been trying but it doesn't make any difference. I just thought it was—I said so to my friend. Of course he made a joke about it and said, 'Why shouldn't Bunny have a woman like any-body else?' " She smiled. "As if any woman would!"

Kersey cross-questioned her for ten minutes without getting any further; the girl was honest; she told what she believed she had seen and she refused to embroider. He said he would send someone to take her statement and that her boy-friend would have to make one as well.

Edward was in his studio-bedroom, a large attic which had once been part of the servants' quarters. An uncurtained dormer window looked out blankly into the night and the room was lit by the yellow light of a naked bulb. There was sisal matting, an easel, an artist's donkey, a table, a superannuated settee and an old armchair. The bedroom component consisted of a single bed and a wardrobe-cup-board.

Canvases were propped face-to-the-wall but one full-length nude —an attenuated Esther—was fastened to the sloping ceiling. Her slimness was exaggerated, diminishing her sex, but the warm flesh tones glowed; a Modigliani version.

Esther and Edward sat side by side on the settee; Esther was turning the pages of a book of reproductions; Edward watched without interest. He was on edge; several times he seemed on the point of speaking but changed his mind, then it came: "I don't know what to do, Esther."

"You don't *have* to do anything, Teddy."

"But when they find her they will know I was her only regular visitor."

"Perhaps they will, but you visit people because you like them; it doesn't mean that you're likely to—"

"The police will know about Father."

"Does that matter? I mean, it would be absurd . . ."

It was all very gentle, words were spoken without emphasis, in sentences which were often incomplete; there was discussion without argument and without urgency; the two of them were like people in someone else's dream.

"They will know that I've been there today."

"How?"

"Because I must have been seen up on the moor."

For the first time Esther showed signs of animation. "You could say that as you were getting near the cottage, on your way home, you saw someone leaving by the back gate."

He looked at her in surprise. "Why should I say that?"

She shook her head and did not answer.

"But who should I say I saw?"

"Anybody—a man."

"But they would want to know what he looked like."

"You could say that you were too far off to see."

Edward looked even more worried. "I don't think they would believe me."

Esther dropped the book to the floor and turned toward him. "Don't worry about it now; think it over."

He slid his hand up under her shirt and caressed her. She remained passive.

"I love your breasts, Esther."

"They're very small."

"I love you, Esther."

"Do you, Teddy?"

Chapter Three

Next morning Wycliffe listened to the seven-o'clock news on the radio. Moscow and Washington were counting missiles as kids count conkers; the French were trying to flog us subsidized oven-ready turkeys and long-life milk while refusing our lamb; trade-union leaders warned darkly of strikes and disruptions if their members failed to get the usual quart out of the pint pot. It was the sort of morning which made him want to get off.

But there was nowhere to escape to, even in a pipe-dream. In Alaska they scrambled for gold and oil while the Eskimos drew social security instead of catching seals and building igloos; in darkest Africa they carried Soviet-made machine-guns and had pictures of Castro in their mud huts; in Outer Mongolia they were joining collectives and attending classes in cultural awareness, while up the Amazon they bulldozed forests and doled out influenza and syphilis to underprivileged little Indians who hadn't known what they were missing.

The moon was the last wilderness and that remained inaccessible even in imagination to a middle-aged copper who was fundamentally unadventurous and only wanted people to be reasonable and decent.

Of course it was raining; the weather had changed overnight, and from the windows of the watch house the estuary looked leaden, like the sky. Inside, for no reason at all, the atmosphere was gloomily tense; one of those mornings.

"What time do I expect you tonight?"

"I've no idea."

"So you won't expect a meal."

"I'll ring you after lunch."

Brittle thread, easily snapped by some pert or hurtful remark, but

Helen was worried about him and came to the door to see him off. She kissed him with a wry smile. "Remember you've got to last till I get another."

He squeezed her arm and everything was right again.

He had got to bed late and slept badly, milling over the day. Some cases hinge on the pathologist's report; others, on what a ballistics expert has to say; sometimes it is highly technical forensic evidence which sets the ball rolling, but in this case the experts had little to offer.

There is not a lot to be said about a shot through the head except that it is usually fatal. (Though Franks had a story about a man who, having shot himself through the temple with a thirty-eight one night, turned up at breakfast next morning.) They had the fatal bullet and the cartridge-case and they knew with reasonable certainty where the gun had come from, but Wycliffe would have been easier in his mind if the gun itself had been recovered.

On reflection, what troubled him most was the passionless, cold-bloodedness of the crime. To lie in wait for someone, then to kill them with a single shot through the skull is as near execution as it is possible to get; a calculated economy of effort which he found profoundly disturbing.

The examination of the victim's clothing had told him little beyond the fact that Bunny had worn long johns and a sleeved woollen vest—both incredibly filthy. He had carried in his pockets seven pounds and sixty-two pence, a few bits of string, a couple of nails and a stub of pencil.

Someone must have worked through the night, for the scene-of-crime report was on his desk. It included a plan of the cottage, all Smith's photographs, and a statement that a complete inventory was under way. Already they had found some money. It seemed that, after all, Emily had "put something by"—one hundred and forty pounds in fives and singles, contained in an old envelope and tucked under Bunny's mattress. Presumably, this was left of a larger sum he had been living on since his mother's death. It wouldn't have kept him for much longer, but if the killer or anyone else had really searched the place it could hardly have been money he was after.

His personal assistant came in with the morning mail. Diane, alias the Ice Maiden, alias the Snow Queen. Diane was like all the "afters" in TV toilet commercials rolled into one; shampooed, conditioned, deodorized, delicately perfumed and exquisitely packaged. She made him feel uncomfortable so that he wondered if he had shaved properly, if he had soap behind his ears, if he smelled of stale tobacco . . .

"Put them there, Diane."

She was as impeccable in her work as in her person. She laid down a pile of envelopes, putting one gingerly apart from the rest. It was a straw-coloured envelope addressed in block capitals to "The Head of Detectives." The classic format. He opened it with a minimum of handling—not that it mattered. Nobody tangling with the police and having an I.Q. of eighty-five plus leaves prints any more. The contents were brief and mandatory: *Find out Edwards reel name.* The envelope was postmarked Newton District, which told him very little. The message, like the address, had been written in carefully formed block capitals by someone not very familiar with the business of writing. Although educated people will often pretend to illiteracy when writing anonymous letters this had the appearance of the genuine article. The paper had been roughly torn from a lined exercise book.

Wycliffe received a dozen anonymous letters a week, mostly from nut-cases, some from neighbours with a grievance, the odd one with a useful tip. The problem was to know one from the other.

Edward's real name. Edward—the painter, the doe-eyed young man who had been so self-effacing the previous afternoon when they met in the churchyard. It would be no surprise to hear that he had suffered some traumatic experience in childhood.

Anyway, there seemed to be a conspiracy to put the Beales in the centre of the stage. The question was, how to proceed. He thought of calling on Simon, then remembered that Maurice would be in the firm's offices in the city. Whether the anonymous query had any significance or not, it would be an excuse to talk to Maurice, whom he had not yet seen.

He sent the note and its envelope up for routine examination and for photocopies to be made, then he put through a call to Beales'

Household Stores and asked to speak to Mr. Maurice Beale. He was politely interrogated.

"Is it a business or a private matter, sir?"

"Private."

"Mr. Wycliffe . . . Would that be Chief Superintendent Wycliffe?"

"It would."

"One moment, Mr. Wycliffe."

Evidently Maurice was not available to any peasant who happened to have a telephone.

One moment stretched into several, then came a high-pitched, slightly irritable voice, not unlike Simon's. "Mr. Wycliffe? You wanted to speak to me?"

"I want to come and see you this morning."

A pause. "This morning? I'm afraid I have a very busy morning ahead of me."

"So have I, Mr. Beale, but this is important."

"I see. Shall we say at ten-thirty, then?"

"Always do your homework!" He said it often enough to earnest young coppers in training and he followed his own precept. He telephoned an accountant friend who sometimes helped him in cases involving finance.

"Beales? I'd say they were riding very comfortably. I doubt if they've even noticed that it's cold outside. . . . Of course, it's a private company—a family concern and in some ways that makes it easier—no beady-eyed shareholders breathing down your neck. . . . About ten years ago Simon had a deed of settlement drawn up; put the capital into a hundred shares and doled them out to the family. As far as I remember he kept about half himself; I think Nicholas, Gertrude and Gertrude's husband—Vicary—got ten each. Something like that anyway. . . . Maurice, as managing director, probably got a few more."

"And who runs the show—Maurice?"

"Maurice? Maurice couldn't run a stall in a church bazaar. Simon inherited a good business and ran it on sound lines, but the real growth has come in the last few years and it's all down to Frank Vicary. He's a natural—pity he can't take over one of our state-subsidized disaster areas. Strange chap, looks a bit like a monkey I always think. . . ."

Wycliffe thanked him.

"Anytime! Love to Helen."

Beales' Household Stores occupied a prime site in the city centre; four floors of merchandise ranging from tin-tacks to power lathes and from nail brushes to complete bathroom and kitchen installations. An assistant escorted Wycliffe to a padded door and a lift which whisked him to the top floor, to a reception desk and a grey-haired lady who told him that he was expected, that Mr. Beale was engaged but would be free shortly, and would Mr. Wycliffe take a seat.

The hub of the Beale empire. A glass partition separated the receptionist from a room full of clerks and typists. Behind her, two doors were labelled respectively, Maurice Beale, Managing Director; Frank Vicary, Secretary and Accountant.

At three minutes turned the half hour Beale came out of his office. "Mr. Wycliffe?" In contrast with his father's spare hardness, Maurice was fleshy and soft and he seemed to be doing his best to smother nervousness with pomposity. "This way, Superintendent." His office was large, modern, and totally lacking in any trace of individuality. Wycliffe was assigned to a black-leather monster of an armchair while Maurice swivelled at his desk and fiddled with a bundle of typescript.

Wycliffe said, "You know that I am investigating the death of Morley Newcombe and the disappearance of your brother's gun."

Beale studied his fingernails. "I really don't see how I can be of any help, Mr. Wycliffe. Of course, as a family, we are very distressed about the whole affair, but each of us has been questioned by one of your men and, no doubt, you will see the reports."

Wycliffe brought out a photostat of the anonymous note and passed it over. Maurice looked at it and became very still, then he said, "What is it you want from me, Superintendent?"

"Simply to ask if you can explain this note which reached me anonymously in the post this morning."

Maurice decided to be peevish. "Am I expected to explain the actions of some anonymous person who is clearly out to cause trouble? It seems that our family is a target for someone who is trying to implicate us in the death of this man. First my brother's gun is stolen, now this. . . . Surely you can see that the very idea is absurd. Why would any of us want to harm Newcombe?"

Why, indeed? What had people in offices like this to do with a dirty little fat man who lived with his chickens and rabbits?

Wycliffe said, "I see your point, Mr. Beale, but there must be a straightforward answer to the question in the note and it's surely better for me to come to you for it than look elsewhere. However . . ." He seemed on the point of getting up to go.

Maurice's plump fingers interlocked. "I'm not so foolish as to refuse an explanation."

The intercom buzzed and Maurice flicked a button with aggression. "I am engaged, Miss Marks. Ask Mr. Yeo to deal with whatever it is." He sat back in his chair, swivelling to and fro. "Rather than have your men ferreting out a garbled version of the facts I had better tell you what this is about and you will see that it can have nothing to do with your case."

Maurice picked up the photostat and studied it once more. Now that he had decided to talk he was going to extract as much drama as possible from the situation. "I suppose all families have their skeleton, tucked away. . . ." He looked at Wycliffe with a depreciating smile. "This is ours. Does the name Santos mean anything to you, Superintendent?—Eduardo Santos?"

"Not that I recall."

"I thought you might remember the case, Eduardo Santos, a painter of Spanish extraction, living in Camden, strangled his wife in somewhat bizarre circumstances. The woman he strangled was my aunt—my mother's younger sister; and, of course, Edward's mother. Edward was eight at the time and he witnessed the whole horrible business."

"What happened to Santos?"

"He got a life sentence for murder."

"Is he still in prison?"

"No, he was released on parole some years ago but there has never been any contact between Edward and his father since, early in his sentence, Santos renounced all claims on his son and the boy was adopted by my father and mother."

"A tragic affair!"

Maurice nodded with lugubrious emphasis. "Yes, indeed! Edward was a charming boy and he is a delightful young man but despite that he has been a great worry to my wife and to me. My mother died seven years ago but before that she was ill for a long time and so it fell mainly to us to bring Edward up."

Maurice stared at his clasped hands. "Through no fault of his own he was a most difficult youngster—his schooldays were a catalogue of illnesses which, according to the doctors, were more of the mind than the body." He looked at Wycliffe with an owlish expression and grew more confiding: "I must confess that my father's attitude didn't help. He is a strong man and, although he is very fond of Edward, he has often shown a lack of understanding. . . . I'm afraid he has little sympathy for weakness of any kind."

Maurice lowered his voice. "During his teens Edward suffered long periods of intense depression and when he was eighteen he attempted suicide on two occasions."

"How?"

The bald enquiry shocked Maurice but he rallied. "On the first occasion he drank weed-killer and on the second, he slashed his wrists."

Maurice sat back in his chair with a deep sigh. "Well, Mr. Wycliffe, now you know the explanation of your anonymous note. I am sure you will see that it can have nothing to do with the case. After all, a young man who has twice tried to kill himself can hardly be thought of as a danger to others."

Evidently Maurice had not read the right books. Wycliffe, who had, retained an interest in Edward but was disinclined to see him as a prime suspect without more evidence. For the moment, enough was enough.

He got up to leave. "Is Mr. Vicary in this morning?"

Mild surprise. "What? No, I'm afraid he's away all day today; he's looking into problems at our Tor Vale depot."

"Isn't that the one on the Newton road?"

"Yes. Actually it's quite close to Washford."

Wycliffe was escorted to the lift. "If I can be of any further help
. . ." A soft hand.

Wycliffe drove back to his headquarters and spent an hour coping
with rosters, schedules, and interdepartmental queries. He dealt
with the routine bumf, both reassured and irritated by Diane standing over him, watching for any slip.

"The chief wants to know when he can expect your comments on
his Emergency Deployment proposals."

His ball-point ran out, he threw it down and groped for another.

"Here!" Diane's ball-points were like the widow's cruse of oil. She
pegged away at him: "Shall I say that you'll let him have something
by the morning?"

He did not answer. It was not that he was wilfully uncooperative
but when anything diverted him from a case in which he was deeply
involved he exhibited what Kersey called "the Zombie Syndrome."
It was something more than mere preoccupation; almost as though
he had assumed a different identity.

At one-fifteen he went out to lunch at his usual restaurant; he was
served by his usual waitress and surrounded by regulars like himself
but for all his awareness he might have been alone. By two o'clock
he was on the motorway out of the city.

Visibility was down to fifty yards but vans, coaches, juggernauts
and cars swished bravely by, firm in their faith in brakes, tyres and
St. Christopher. Wycliffe had no such faith and he was glad when
he reached the turn-off, free to meander in peace.

The road snaked through a narrow wooded valley; mist blotted
out everything above ten or fifteen feet but at ground level it was
clear. A sign by the road announced Tor Vale; the valley broadened
to make room for a few cottages and the Tor Vale Hotel. A discreet
sign pointed into the trees: Tor Vale Cash and Carry Depot. He had
decided to call on Vicary. The depot, a barracks of concrete and
asbestos, mercifully shielded by trees, was built on three sides of a
car-park and dignified only by a four-storey stone building which had
once been a flour mill. The way in led him to a turnstyle and a
sergeant-major type wearing a security badge.

"Mr. Vicary? Straight on through Footwear and Clothing into

Gardening, then up the stairs to a door marked Private. Knock on that."

It worked, producing a plump blonde who said, "I'll see."

Two minutes later he was in a large, bare office where everything was basic. Vicary was saying to a man in a grey overall with a "Manager" badge, "Come back in fifteen minutes."

Vicary was small, with a boyish figure, but he had a heavily lined face which made him look old as well as somewhat simian. He had a wide mouth and his smile was more like a grimace.

"Ah, Mr. Wycliffe! I was expecting to hear from you sometime but I hardly thought you would search me out here."

No voluptuous armchairs, only the bentwood kitchen variety— from stock. They sat down, Vicary on one side of the desk, Wycliffe on the other.

"I've just come from talking to your brother-in-law at the store, he told me I should find you here. I wanted to ask how well you knew Newcombe."

The grey eyes looked straight at Wycliffe. "I suppose the short answer is: well enough to know that he was an unpleasant bit of work. While his mother was alive she kept him out of trouble."

"Trouble which has now got him shot?"

A faint smile. "I certainly didn't expect that. I regarded Newcombe as a layabout, perhaps a small-time crook, but not interesting enough to get himself shot."

"Did you have much contact with him?"

A canny look; it was not difficult to see why Frank Vicary, clerk, had become Simon Beale's son-in-law and virtual boss of the firm. "I went to see him on Sunday afternoon as, I suspect, you already know. It will save time and, hopefully, complications if I tell you about it."

Wycliffe waited while the executive mind switched from stock control to an orderly recall of the events in question, suitably edited.

"Newcombe's father and mother both worked at Ashill and my father-in-law paid the widow a fairly generous pension. When she died, a few months ago, he allowed the payments to continue as a gesture to the son. It was made clear that this was a temporary arrangement to enable him to get on his feet, and last Sunday I had the job of telling him that it would finish at the end of the month."

Wycliffe quoted: " 'You've done very well out of this, Newcombe, but there's a limit; all good things come to an end some time.' "

Vicary laughed, and his face seemed to split in two; no doubt at school he had acquired an apt nickname. "You are very well informed, Mr. Wycliffe! I certainly said something like that. The man was a sponger and if I'd had my way the cut-off would have come much sooner."

"I think you went on to say: 'If you adopt that attitude, Newcombe, you are making the biggest mistake of your life.' "

Did the eyes show a little more concern? If so it was gone in an instant and the explanation came, pat: "That sounds a bit more suggestive, doesn't it?—in the circumstances. In fact, it was in answer to a remark of Newcombe's which sounded very much like a threat."

"A threat?"

"It seems absurd, I know, but he really was a most unpleasant creature. He said that if he talked to my father-in-law he thought he would do better."

"And you saw that as a threat?"

"He meant it as one."

"But what hold did he think he had over Mr. Beale?"

"I haven't the least idea and I didn't enquire."

Wycliffe said, easily, "He was obviously not a very intelligent man. A few days before he was killed he went to Newton register office and asked to see three entries in the records."

"Indeed?" Vicary's manner seemed to show only polite interest.

"The first concerned the details of his own birth; the second, your marriage to Gertrude Beale; and the third, the birth of your daughter, Esther."

Vicary was looking straight at Wycliffe and his expression did not change. He said, simply, "How very odd! I wonder what he hoped to gain by that?"

Wycliffe said, "A simple question, Mr. Vicary: was he blackmailing you, or hoping to do so?"

A grim smile. "He certainly wasn't blackmailing me, Mr.

Wycliffe; I can't answer for what he was hoping to do but if he had
any idea of the sort I can't imagine what grounds he thought he
had."

Wycliffe stood up. "Thank you. I won't take up any more of your
time."

The depot manager was outside the door, waiting to be recalled.

Wycliffe made his way back through Gardening, Clothing and
Footwear—past stacks of consumer goods, waiting to be consumed.
Multiply that by tens of thousands. . . . It bothered him sometimes; on the other hand he didn't fancy the idea of queuing outside
a British version of GUM for the privilege of buying whatever an
omniscient state had decided was good for him.

Vicary's story of the pension could be true—it probably was; people like Vicary rarely told outright lies, but it was not the whole
truth. He was dealing with a specialist in processing and packaging
truth with a deceptive label. And blackmail? It had to be considered.

Washford looked very different from the day before; the moor was
obliterated and the village seemed about to dissolve in a moist grey-
ness, half drizzle, half fog. Colours had vanished, leaving a circum-
scribed landscape in monochrome.

Three or four police cars were parked by the incident van but the
doings of the police were overshadowed by greater activity in the
field adjoining the churchyard. Here there were other, more garish
caravans; large, box-like trailers and ancient diesels to tow them, and
to double as generators when the fun-fair got under way. The fair
had come to town and when the fair comes to town, it rains—a law
of Nature which Wycliffe had learned as a small boy.

Despite the weather, men were busy erecting stalls and booths,
rides and roundabouts. Already the skeletal frameworks of a helter-
skelter and a big-wheel reached jaggedly skywards, and other struc-
tures were taking shape, not yet identifiable.

The church clock chimed and struck three. From the school came
a man's voice, strictly admonishing his class. As Wycliffe was getting
out of his car Nicholas came through the gates of Ashill. He wore a
shabby raincoat and a fisherman's hat but he stalked along with such

bearing and precision of step that one listened instinctively for bugles and drums. He looked neither to the right nor to the left and, if he saw Wycliffe, he gave no sign. He crossed the Green and entered the churchyard by the lich-gate.

Kersey was in the police van.

"I was going back to Newton but I heard on the grape-vine that you were on the way, so I waited."

The movements of senior police officers are monitored with as much care and in as much detail as those of known criminals believed to be on a job.

"There was a message from the coroner's office; it seems the Fretwells are anxious to bury Newcombe on Thursday and the coroner wants to know if we have any objection. I told him to go ahead unless he heard different from you this afternoon."

"The Fretwells are in a hurry, aren't they?"

Kersey grinned. "Get him under before the fair so that everybody can enjoy themselves."

Wycliffe said, "Anything else?"

Kersey pointed to a stout cardboard box on the table. "You might like to take a look in there, sir."

Wycliffe removed the lid and lifted out an official police inventory tag. Underneath were two wads of old "white" five-pound notes, tightly rolled and secured by a piece of thread; and three linen bags, tubular in form, each with a draw-string top.

"You needn't bother to open them if you don't want to, sir; each of 'em contains sovereigns and half-sovereigns. It's all listed on the tag but the total is sixty sovereigns and eighty half-sovereigns."

"Where did you find that lot?"

"Smith found it. You remember the old brass bed in Emily's bedroom?"

"I do; my grandparents had one like it."

"I'll bet theirs didn't have a small fortune stowed away under the knobs."

"Any idea of what it amounts to in value?"

Kersey shook his head. "I suppose the fivers carry only their face value and there are a hundred and three of them. I haven't a clue about the gold but it must be quite a packet. I suppose we hold it in the station safe until—"

"For the moment, but notify the legal department and let them handle it; they'll probably contact the Fretwells' lawyer, and one way or another, they'll nominate somebody to wind up the estate."

Wycliffe put the cover back on the box. "I suppose she bought the gold before the restrictions in the middle sixties."

Kersey said, "I wish I'd bought gold in the sixties; the snag was I didn't have any more to buy it with than I have now. Do you think this is what the killer was after?"

"If it was he made a hash of it. In any case it doesn't make sense. Newcombe's movements were known to the whole village and any intruder could have picked his time to make a leisurely search without fear of interruption. In fact, he made sure of being there when Newcombe returned, which seems to clinch it as premeditated murder."

Kersey agreed. "That's what it looks like."

"Any more surprises?"

Kersey shrugged. "It's got about that the gun which killed him came from Ashill and the house-to-house chaps say the attitudes of the villagers have changed. Yesterday they were chatty, glad to gossip; full of yarns about Newcombe. It seems he had an amorous side, if you can call it that; he used to accost girls and make obscene suggestions. Nobody bothered about it much; all good clean bucolic fun, but at least they told us. Today they've clammed up; all you can get is abuse of the Beales. The feeling against the family is pretty strong and to listen to some you'd think all we had to do was take a Beale and truss him up ready for the pot."

"Which? Have they any preference?"

"I don't think they're bothered about trifles like that."

Wycliffe thought he had read the signs the day before but Kersey was having to learn about village ways—in real villages, not suburban dormitories or second-home reservations which are only villages in name.

Kersey said, "Unless something happens soon I think we and the Beales are in for plenty of stick."

Wycliffe brought him up to date on his interviews with Maurice and with Vicary.

"You think there could be something in the blackmail angle?"

Wycliffe grimaced. "It's possible I suppose, but these people— Simon, Vicary, even Maurice—they're business people; their job consists in wheeling and dealing, bluff and counterbluff. If New- combe was trying to squeeze them on the strength of some family skeleton they'd bamboozle him with tactics and tie him up so tight he'd be afraid to squeak, but I don't think they'd shoot him."

Kersey sighed. "Somebody did."

Wycliffe ticked off points, mentally. "You've got a statement from the Gratton girl?"

"Yes; it doesn't tell us anything fresh. I don't think there's much in it but I suppose we should try to be sure. If the weather is good enough we could have a rerun tonight—a couple of fellows and a couple of women; put her on the seat and see what she makes of it. At least we might get some idea of what she did see."

"I agree."

Wycliffe telephoned his headquarters: "Telex to the Met: Details of wife-murder: Eduardo Santos in Camden, approximately fourteen years ago. Santos released on parole—details."

The duty officer brought in an official envelope. "Just arrived from Newton subdivision, sir."

He slit open the envelope and spread the contents on the little table for Kersey to see. Copies of two certificates, one recording the marriage of Francis Arthur Vicary to Gertrude Rosemary Beale on January 2, 1962; the other, the birth of their child, Esther Gertrude, on August 4 in the same year.

Kersey said, "So what? A seven-month baby? More likely careless premarital sex, but either way, what can we make of it?"

Wycliffe growled. "I'm damned if I know; the point is, what had Newcombe expected, or hoped for?"

He sat back in his chair, filled his pipe and lit it. Kersey, envious, said, "I thought you were cutting down."

"I am; this is only the second today."

Wycliffe smoked in silence while Kersey turned over the pages of the report file. The church clock chimed a quarter to four and almost at once a bell sounded somewhere in the school. Within a minute, children were tumbling through the gates and fanning out over the Green; interest now, focused on the fair.

Wycliffe said, "Naomi and Maurice have probably been married for twenty years at least."

"So?"

He seemed about to offer some explanation but changed his mind and said only: "I think I'll talk to her."

"Do you want me any more, sir?"

"No."

"Then I'll get back to the office. My sergeant will think I've gone away to live."

Wycliffe smiled to himself. Kersey was getting a kick out of his promotion.

"How long have you been married, Mrs. Beale?"

Naomi looked at him, unsure whether or not she should treat the question as impertinent; but she answered, "Twenty-one years. Maurice and I were rather young—"

He cut her short, thinking that she might be more helpful if she was slightly confused. "So you were here for a long time with Emily Newcombe."

She amended that promptly: "Emily worked here for seventeen or eighteen years after my marriage."

"Part time?"

"Part time, full time—as she wanted it. She and Joyce were as thick as thieves and they worked it to suit themselves. My father-in-law was absurdly indulgent to them—as he still is to Joyce. And that makes for problems in running the house, I can tell you!"

They were in a tiny room, hardly more than a cubby-hole, which Naomi called her "retreat." It had a writing-table and chair, two armchairs and a shelf stacked with women's magazines; there was no room for more. She had said, "We shall be more private in here."

"So you were already established at Ashill when your sister-in-law married Mr. Vicary and, of course, when their child was born."

She was clearly puzzled by these remarks which were not quite questions and seemed inconsequential. After starting a sentence she thought better of it and said nothing.

Wycliffe spoke conversationally, almost dreamily; he had relaxed into his chair and seemed to have all the time in the world. With no particular aim he was offering Naomi a variety of baits, any one of which might draw her into talk.

"I saw your husband this morning and he was telling me about the tragic events which brought Edward to live here and how most of the responsibility for the boy fell upon you."

"Maurice told you that?" Her sharp little eyes scanned his placid features in surprise. "Well, it's no more than the simple truth."

"Of course, your mother-in-law was alive for several years after Edward's arrival. I suppose it was only after her death—"

She cut him short. "Edward came here when he was eight and he was thirteen when my mother-in-law died, but for those five years she was a virtual invalid; she had a heart condition and we had to be careful not to excite her. . . . It was very difficult because I had the responsibility without the authority." Naomi's cheeks flushed as she recalled her frustrations.

"Your mother-in-law had different ideas about Edward's upbringing?"

Naomi laughed briefly. "They were Ruby Price's ideas; that's what made it so . . . so galling."

"Ruby Price?"

"She was the district nurse—a glorified midwife. She's been retired for years now, but she still lives in Washford."

"She had some influence over your mother-in-law?"

Naomi hesitated, but the chance to unburden some of the accumulated bitterness of years was too much for her; and this man, policeman though he was, had a quiet sympathetic manner which made it easy to talk to him. She said, "I'd put it stronger than that; my mother-in-law was *dominated* by Ruby Price!" The tiny, rather pathetic little mouth trembled. "Whatever that woman said was right." She studied the rings on her plump fingers, then looked up at him. "Do you know, all three children—Maurice, Nicholas and Gertrude—were brought into the world by Ruby Price—in this house. Any other woman of her class would have gone into a nursing home and had the best of everything. Even when Gertrude had Esther, it was Ruby Price . . . I said to Gertrude at the time, 'If it were me . . . !' "

"But she fell in with her mother's wishes?"

"She—" Naomi stopped herself. "Well, that's another story."

"I would have thought that the husband—Mr. Vicary—would have had something to say."

Naomi gave an unpleasant little laugh. "Her husband! You've got to remember that Frank Vicary was very small fry then—scarcely believing in his luck! He wasn't secretary-accountant in those days!"

"So that Edward was a teenager before you were in a position to—"

She cut him short. "Edward, poor boy, was never given a chance. My father-in-law took against him almost from the moment his wife died. . . . If I'm truthful, I should say that he was *turned* against the boy."

"By whom?"

A knowing smile. "Who do you think? Simon was disappointed at not having a grandson and there was just the possibility that he might have thought of Edward as a substitute. . . . Frank Vicary wasn't going to have that!"

"I would have thought Simon Beale a very difficult man to influence."

"So he is—by anybody other than his famous son-in-law!"

She broke off abruptly, listening to some sound which Wycliffe had missed. Almost at once there was a tap at the door which opened, and Joyce was standing there. It seemed obvious that Naomi felt she had been caught out.

"What is it, Joyce?" Snappish.

"You haven't said anything about vegetables for tonight."

Chapter Four

Mist over the estuary and before he was properly awake Wycliffe could hear the booming of a fog-horn down the coast like the lowing of a cow in labour. The radio promised that the mists would clear, that the sun would break through to give a fine, dry day.

"Take your mack, just in case . . ."

Wycliffe was at his desk by eight, ready for any of his pigeons which might come home to roost. The first was a telex from the Met: "Eduardo Santos, convicted of wife-murder November sixty-eight. Sentenced life: paroled March seventy-seven. Since lived with sister, Islington. Advise further details or action."

Another, a report from Ballistics, seemed to clinch the provenance of the gun which had killed Newcombe: "Scratches on the cartridge-case produced by the ejector mechanism closely resemble those on photographic record of the experimental firing of similar ammunition from a nine-millimetre Beretta M951. The steel, as opposed to the unsatisfactory alloy version of this pistol, was first available in 1955 and was marketed commercially under the trade name Brigadier . . ."

The file on the case was getting fatter but hardly more enlightening. A middle-aged layabout, a bachelor living alone, had been shot through the head one night with a very professional weapon. This, in a village of a thousand people where crime with a capital C was virtually unknown; a closely knit community where it was soon common knowledge if husband and wife decided on twin beds or a new washing-machine. The only outsiders were the Beales, isolated by their money, their religion, their patronage, and the high wall round Ashill. Now it was certain that the gun used by the killer had come from there.

With the ball-point he was holding Wycliffe wrote the word MO-

TIVE on his scribbling pad and underlined it three times. What had made this middle-aged, verminous yokel a target for the killer?

When Diane arrived he said, "Find out if Sergeant Willis is in the building and, if he is, ask him to come here."

Willis worked in the drugs squad but Wycliffe remembered that he was a do-it-yourself fanatic, what used to be called a home handyman, and Beales had a department which was the Mecca of that breed.

Willis was nearing retirement, counting the days, having had his fill of the most depressing and unrewarding job in the force, where the kicks come from both sides, villains and victims. Willis arrived, a massively built man who looked as though he had been hewn from the solid and allowed to weather.

"I suppose you are a customer in the D.I.Y. department at Beales?"

"Have been for years, sir."

"Do you deal with anybody in particular? Anybody you prefer to go to?"

A flicker of interest but no questions. "They're a helpful lot and their prices are competitive, that's why people go there, but there was one chap I used to know especially well. He's retired now— hung up his overall and collected his clock a year ago."

"He sounds like the chap I'm after."

"Billy Reynolds? What's he done?"

"Nothing that I know of but I want somebody who can tell me about the firm as it was twenty years ago."

Willis laughed. "Billy will do that all right, it's his hobby-horse. He worked there from leaving school."

"Do you know where he lives?"

"I do, as it happens, sir. As far as I know he's still got the same house in Coronation Terrace out to Havercombe. I can't tell you the number. . . ."

Wycliffe would have liked to talk to Billy himself but there are limits.

"Have you got much on at the moment?"

"Nothing that can't wait."

"You've heard of Frank Vicary?"

"I know he's a director of Beales and that he married the boss's daughter."

"Good! I want you to go and see Reynolds; find out all you can about Vicary; especially about his early days with the firm and his marriage to Gertrude Beale. It must have caused enough gossip at the time. Tell Reynolds we shall treat what he tells us in confidence."

Willis said, "Is it the Washford murder?"

"Yes, and you'd better report direct to me or to Mr. Kersey—at Washford."

Later that morning, when he arrived in Washford, there was more evidence of hardening attitudes in the village. Some creative artist with an aerosol paint can had sprayed the word MURDERERS across the mellow brickwork of the wall in front of Ashill. An old man, presumably their gardener, was trying to get it off with some sort of solvent, and a free-lance photographer of Wycliffe's acquaintance was taking pictures, making sure that the police van was included. So far the press and TV had shown little interest in Washford's murder but anything might trigger them off.

Kersey was in the van, going through house-to-house reports and marking the interesting bits with a red ball-point.

Wycliffe asked him about the Nancy Gratton experiment: "Did it come off?"

Kersey grinned. "The girl cooperated and we went through the drill but I doubt if it got us any further. We tried her with two women and two men, in random order, making twenty appearances, with sometimes a hand torch and sometimes a candle. She got the sex right thirteen out of the twenty times. I don't know what the statisticians would make of that but I do know that the seat is a long way from the window and with the dim light of a candle or torch . . ." Kersey screwed up his rubbery features in a grimace. "I don't think we can rely too much on Nancy."

Wycliffe said, "Anything else?"

"Just something in the reports: gossip about old Blatchford, the innkeeper. It seems he's a widower and that his late wife was sister to Joyce, the old girl who works at Ashill. The word is that he now sleeps with Dora who's less than half his age and not at all bad to

look at." Kersey was mildly envious. "I'd like to think that at seventy
. . . But maybe it's the pub she's after. And speaking of the pub,
there's something else. The Blatchfords have been there for generations; they had the place on a lease from the Ashill estate, but when
Simon took over he gave them notice to quit. At that time our
Blatchford was working as a sales rep for a firm of agricultural merchants and his parents were running the pub. The story goes that he
went to Simon and threatened to expose some fiddle over govern-
ment subsidies on the estate farms. As a result the Blatchfords were
allowed to buy their freehold."

The same sort of tales had circulated endlessly in Wycliffe's village; they were part of the folklore; whether they were true or not
scarcely mattered.

Wycliffe was staring out of the window at Ashill. "That damned
wall!"

"The wall? You mean who's been writing on it?"

"I mean the wall; they hide behind it. In a way, the villagers have
a point. If the Beales hadn't been who they are we should have gone
a long way towards sorting them out by now. But we daren't cut
corners; if we do we shall be tripping over lawyers from then on.
Before we can tackle any one of them we've got to have a case that
hangs together—and that means we've got to have a motive."

Kersey said, "You seem sure they've got the answer."

Wycliffe glanced at him and away again without comment. After
a moment he said: "They don't live their entire lives in there; Maurice and Vicary go to their office; Edward sells his pictures—he must
have an agent, a gallery or something. What about the others?
What do they do? They must have friends, acquaintances, interests.
. . . Don't tell me that Nicky, for example, spends all his time
cultivating his moustache and playing at soldiers."

Kersey said, "You want them filled out; I see that. But it won't be
easy to make the kind of inquiries you're after without stirring
things."

"Then let's stir."

While the two men were talking there had been almost continuous exchanges on the radio next door; occasionally involving the
duty officer, whose natural voice sounded oddly out of place amid

the bursts of canned speech. It was so ordinary and unremarkable that they had taken no notice but now the duty officer tapped on the door and came in with his message pad.

"Message from P.C. Miller, sir, on his personal radio. He's at Tower Cottage, Vicarage Road, on house-to-house and he's found a dead woman in an upstair room. He says she's been shot."

Wycliffe had an odd feeling; it was as though he had been waiting for this with no real idea of what to expect. He said: "Presumably Miller knows the woman—what's her name?"

The duty officer glanced at his pad. "Price—Ruby Price."

"The midwife?"

The officer looked surprised. "Well, yes, sir. Miller says she's a retired district nurse."

"All right. You know what to do. First, a G.P., then Headquarters; they'll notify the coroner and get things organized."

They looked up Vicarage Road on the map. It branched off from the main street near the top and ran along the upper boundary of the churchyard, above the vicarage; finally it petered out in a lane serving two or three farms. Wycliffe followed Kersey out to his car and they drove up North Street. Vicarage Road began as a double row of terraced houses which were followed by a string of pre-1914 villas in their own gardens; after that, the wall of the churchyard on one side and fields on the other.

Kersey said, "Have we passed the place?"

But when they came to it Tower Cottage was not easily missed: it looked like a little church which had been domesticated and it stood in a garden behind a privet hedge. A stile on each side of the road marked the line of the footpath to the moor which skirted the grounds of the vicarage on one side and followed the line of the privet hedge on the other.

Miller was waiting for them just inside the gate. "This way, sir." He led the way to the back door. "She never used the front."

A ginger cat padded about the yard, mewing piteously. Miller said, "It was up there with her; I had to shut it out." He pushed open the door, fending off the cat while they entered the kitchen. Music came from somewhere upstairs and Miller said, "It's her radio—I didn't think I ought to touch anything."

An electric cooker and refrigerator at least thirty years old, and shelves stacked with preserving jars and bottles; everything gleaming clean but an overall yeasty smell. Miller pointed to a couple of glass jars popping into their airlocks, "She makes her own wine."

Beyond the kitchen, a tiny hall and a staircase—more like a mill-ladder—which led to the upper room. Wycliffe went up alone. At the top of the stairs he was able to look into a large, square room with two windows, one facing the moor and the other looking out over the village. Despite the gloom and drizzle outside the room was bright and cheering. On the radio a choir was singing the hymn "Ye Holy Angels Bright."

The dead woman lay in a heap on the floor by the window which overlooked the moor; her body was partly supported by a wicker chair and she was surrounded by bits of china and a tea-tray which must have been knocked over as she slid from the chair to the floor. She had been shot through the head. Wycliffe did not go into the room. Between him and the dead woman a round, cast-iron stove stood on its iron tray and sent a smoke-pipe up through the ceiling. The tray was littered with paper, some of it burned to ash, some scorched and charred.

Nothing to do but wait for the experts.

"You have been listening to morning service broadcast from the church of St. Michael and All Angels. . . ." The cultured voice of the woman presenter spoke blindly into the room.

He went downstairs and was joined by Kersey and Miller in the garden. "How did you find her?"

Miller said, "She's a Miss Ruby Price, sir. I was on house-to-house —actually, she was the last call on my list. I went to the back door, which was open, and knocked. I know she's a bit deaf and I could hear music coming from somewhere so I called out. After two or three goes I got concerned so I went through the kitchen to the bottom of the stairs and shouted from there. Of course, there was no answer, so I thought I'd better find out if anything was wrong. . . ."

"She lived here alone?"

"Most of her life I think, sir. She was the district nurse till she

retired and that must have been way back. She was quite a character
—well known for miles around."

Wycliffe had the absurd notion that he was being "let in" on the
plot a stage at a time; only the previous day he had first heard of
Ruby Price from Naomi; and probably at that time she was already
dead, shot through the head, as Newcombe had been.

The sound of a car stopping came from the road.

"See who it is, Miller."

Wycliffe walked down the back garden, a series of neatly culti-
vated, weed-free plots in the black earth: potatoes, broad beans,
carrots, parsnips, runner beans under cloches. . . . The bottom
end of the garden was given over to fruit trees and here there was a
gate opening onto the footpath which led to the moor. At this point
the path ran along the edge of a field where sheep were grazing;
beyond that other tiny fields, then the open moor, and finally the
twin tors on the skyline.

Miller came back with the doctor, a man in his sixties, stout and
florid; a physician in need of a spot of self-healing if only by cutting
down on the whisky.

He spoke to Kersey: "You're keeping me busy; two in as many
days is a bit much for a village this size."

Kersey introduced him to Wycliffe. "Dr. Sharpe, Detective Chief
Superintendent Wycliffe."

Wycliffe went upstairs with the doctor and into the room for the
first time.

Sharpe went straight to the body and bent over it. "Poor old
Ruby! To finish up like this! What are we dealing with, Mr.
Wycliffe—a homicidal maniac?" A moment later he went on,
"Well, you don't need me to tell you she's dead. Shot through the
head, the same as Newcombe." He looked at his watch as though it
might help him. "She's been dead a good while; long enough for
rigor to come and go. . . . She's been there since yesterday at least,
possibly before that, but Franks will tell you. After all, he's paid for
it."

Wycliffe switched off the radio; he was looking round the room
with curiosity but unwilling to disturb anything until his blood-
hounds had sniffed it over. Apart from the cast-iron stove, which

reminded him of the one in his classroom when he started school, there were a large work-table, an old treadle sewing machine, two worn armchairs which did not match, cupboards and bookshelves. The floor was covered with sisal matting strewn with homemade woollen rugs.

"Can you tell me anything about her, Doctor?"

The doctor fingered his gingery moustache which was turning grey. "Depends what you want to know. I looked in on her now and then for old times' sake; she never needed me professionally, she was tough as old boots. I suppose you know she was our district nurse until she retired ten or twelve years back? She covered the same ground as I do. She must be seventy-four or -five now but she very nearly lived off what she grew herself. She was a dedicated vegetarian; she even thought she'd converted her cat till she found he was catching young rabbits and field-mice on the sly, and that was a great disappointment to her."

"She never married?"

"No. Ruby had very little use for men. She knew her job and she was a worker. When I came here first she was doing her rounds in an old Morgan three-wheeler which she called Boanerges, but before that she had a bike."

The doctor sighed. "She and I attended scores of deliveries together in the old days—all winds and weathers, day and night. Of course that was before the Nye Bevan circus started up, when women still had their babies at home."

"Did she have many visitors?"

"Very few I'd say; she didn't encourage people to come and see her though that didn't stop her visiting them. She kept in touch with 'my mothers and babies,' as she called them, though some of the mothers are dead and gone and a few of the babies must be knocking fifty." He pushed back his fisherman's hat to scratch his thinning hair. "Come to think of it, she did have one regular visitor —young Beale—Edward. Simon adopted him when he was seven or eight—I think he comes from Simon's wife's side. Ruby was very friendly with Simon's wife, who died a few years back, and she always had a fancy for Edward—Teddy, she called him. He seems a bit of an oddity—he's taken up painting and spends a lot of time on the moor sketching, so whenever he's passing he looks in on Ruby."

Wycliffe saw the doctor to his car; then, from his own car, he radioed instructions for more men and more back-up facilities. Whether they would be of any use was a question but the key principle of modern police work is saturation: cast your net wide and often; collect and collate. Gather enough data and what you are looking for is sure to be there somewhere—if only you can find it. Sometimes it works; just as often the culprit is caught—if at all— because of somebody's hunch or through sheer luck—as with the Yorkshire Ripper.

A homicidal maniac the doctor had said, but he was an old-fashioned doctor; we no longer have maniacs, homicidal or otherwise; they have gone the way of idiots, imbeciles and lunatics. Soon criminals will be the "socially maladjusted" but, for the moment, we do have psychopaths who sometimes take to killing people. At some stage he would have to make up his mind whether he was looking for a "killer" in the abstract—a psychopath—or a killer with a motive which might be considered rational.

Sergeant Smith arrived with his photographic gear. "The others are following in the Range Rover, sir." He went upstairs and began putting Ruby's upper room on film. A few minutes later Franks roared up in his Porsche.

"If it goes on like this, Charles, I shall apply for a full-time appointment. Where is he? Or is it a she this time?"

The room with the two windows was beginning to lose its private character as an extension of the dead woman's individuality and was becoming a public place.

Franks said, "Shot like the other. I suppose this one is down to the same gentleman who disposed of Monday's offering?" He turned the body over and Smith's camera recorded his every move. "She's been here for a while, Charles—quite a while, that's for sure." He stood up, dusting off his trousers. "Well, shift her when you like; the sooner the better. Is the van here yet?"

It was another quarter of an hour before the mortuary van arrived with two men who removed what was left of Ruby Price on a canvas stretcher.

Wycliffe's own men took over to begin the business of searching and recording. Wycliffe himself prowled about, looking vaguely at the things with which Ruby had chosen to surround herself and hoping they might tell him something of the kind of woman she was. The bookshelves first. Apart from nursing manuals and works on obstetrics and midwifery—all somewhat dated—there were books on gardening, on the lives of musicians, on vegetarian diets and cookery, and two whole shelves of detective novels. Then the pictures: part of one wall was covered with snapshots of babies, framed in sets of six and each labelled with a name and date. The series covered nearly forty years, from the beginning of the thirties to the late sixties. So Ruby had taken her camera on post-natal visits. The Beales were there with the rest: Nicholas, Maurice and Gertrude and, much later, Esther. There were other framed photographs on the walls, two or three of Ruby herself, and one, taken on the lawn at Ashill, showed a younger Simon, sitting next to a fair, frail-looking woman, a faded English rose. No doubt this was Rosemary. They sat in wicker chairs and there was a third, empty chair, and a little table laden with tea things. Presumably Ruby was taking the picture.

On the same wall as the snapshots of babies there was an oil-painting of the moor in winter, signed E. Beale. The tors were streaked with snow, and blue-black clouds against a bleached sky threatened more to come. The foreground was a study in sombre purples and browns, cunningly slashed with white. Not a comfortable painting; no Christmas card snow-scene. Wycliffe told himself it was a competent piece of work, that it conveyed a powerful sense of loneliness. Charlie Wycliffe: art critic. Success for Helen, who had taken in hand his aesthetic development when they married. At that time he had known little that was not inside the covers of police manuals and law books. Now he knew the difference between a Monet and a Manet; he could distinguish between Mozart and Haydn, and had read Dostoevsky.

The first job of the searchers was to find the cartridge-case belonging to the bullet which had killed Ruby; after that they would look for the bullet itself, which might be embedded in the woodwork or even in a wall.

On the wall opposite the one with the snapshots there were three built-in cupboards and the door of one of them stood a little open. Wycliffe peered in and saw a cardboard box containing a large number of manilla envelopes, stuffed with papers, all standing on edge in the box as though in a filing drawer. From this cupboard a trail of papers led across the floor to the stove, suggesting that Ruby's filing system had been raided and its contents partly destroyed.

Nothing could be done until Smith had checked all likely surfaces for prints, so Wycliffe went downstairs and out to his car.

Outside a group of people had gathered, a dozen or so adults and a couple of children. They stood, silent in the sunshine, looking at nothing, for there was nothing to see except the parked cars. Wycliffe had the impression that they were in some way organized, at least that they had a common purpose beyond merely gawping at the comings and goings. There were no shouts, nothing in the nature of a demonstration, but he sensed their antagonism.

So far, press, radio and television had virtually ignored the murder of Bunny Newcombe, but two killings would make them think again. "Killer Loose in Moorland Village." And it wouldn't be long before someone remembered that this was Baskerville country, though it was hard to imagine a hound operating with a nine-milli-metre automatic.

He drove slowly back to the police caravan. He felt reasonably sure that he was not dealing with the doctor's homicidal maniac, nor with the modern equivalent, a psychopath. In these killings there was nothing to suggest that the killer had taken pleasure in his task —that he had achieved any catharsis through violence. There can hardly be a less spectacular way of achieving sudden death than by a shot through the head. But if the killings had some sort of rational motive, what was the link? Again he was back to the Beales.

Franks had said that Ruby had been dead "quite a while"; exactly how long was important but he would have nothing better to go on until after the post-mortem—if then. In the meantime the obvious thing was to talk to the one member of the Beale family who was known to have kept up contact with the dead woman—Edward.

He parked the car by the police van. On the Green they were stringing rows of flags and fairy lamps between the trees and erecting a wooden platform near the war memorial in preparation for the fair on Friday. The fun-fair was ready for business and due to open that evening.

The church clock chimed and struck three, reminding him that he had had no lunch. Too late now. As he was about to go into the van he saw Esther coming across from Ashill towards him. She was wearing another of her "Impressionist" frocks, a small flower pattern on a white ground, with plenty of tucks and ruching.

"I've been watching for you." She looked at him but her face and manner gave no clue as to whether she had come to discuss Newcombe's rabbits or to tell him of some new tragedy.

"My cousin, Edward, has something to tell you."

Once more he had the feeling that he was playing a role in some drama of which he had not seen the script; it made him uneasy. "Then why doesn't he come here?"

"He's very upset; I had difficulty enough in getting him to let me come."

"What's it about?"

"Ruby Price."

"What about her?"

"You'd better talk to him."

Wycliffe recalled his encounter with Edward in the churchyard. The young man had struck him as timid—perhaps more than timid —scared; but that was on Monday, two days ago.

"If you are going to talk to him you had better come through our flat, otherwise you will have to face Grandfather or Aunt Naomi." She had the devastating frankness of a child with the poise of an adult and he felt like anything but a high-ranking officer conducting an inquiry.

"All right."

He followed her through the gates and round the house to an outside staircase which led to the Vicarys' first-floor flat. In the hall, she said, "Don't make too much noise, I think Mother is asleep."

One of the doors off the hall took them through into the main part of the house, at the end of the first-floor corridor. He followed her, almost the length of the broad corridor, past the head of the staircase, then up a narrow, steep flight of stairs.

"These are the attics where the servants used to sleep when there were proper servants. Edward has the biggest as a studio and bedroom."

Esther opened one of several doors in the long passage of bare boards. It was a large room with a dormer window facing north and even on this sunny afternoon it was filled with a clear, cold, clinical light. Edward was standing by the window looking like a man in the condemned cell. The room was poorly furnished: a bed, a wardrobe, a worn settee and an old armchair; these, and the tools of his trade: easel, painting-table, artist's donkey. . . . There were shelves of art books and a number of canvases stacked face to the wall but nothing on show.

"Mr. Beale?" Wycliffe held out his hand.

He was given the armchair while Edward and Esther sat side by side on the settee and reminded Wycliffe of the babes in the wood.

"You want to tell me something?"

Edward, hollow-eyed and tense, made a couple of false starts before words came properly. "I know about Ruby Price . . . I wanted to tell you that she and I . . . that I usually call there when I'm up on the moor sketching . . . I'm often up there when the weather is fine enough."

"Do you call on her every time you go up to the moor?"

"Almost every time."

"Going or coming back?"

"Usually coming back; in the mornings I like to catch the light." Edward had both hands tucked under his thighs and he was swaying slightly.

"When did you last call?"

A long silence and Wycliffe repeated the question.

"The day before yesterday—Monday." The words were only barely audible.

"When you last saw her, was she her usual self?"

"She was dead." Edward heaved a great sigh as though a burden had fallen from his shoulders.

Esther sat bolt upright, never showing any sign of involvement; in her old-fashioned dress she could have been posing for a photograph.

Wycliffe sounded a note of caution, as much for his own sake as Edward's.

"Remember you are volunteering information."

"I want to tell you about it."

"Very well. Did you kill her?"

"No!"

"She was dead when you found her?"

"Yes."

"When was that?"

"Sometime before five o'clock on Monday afternoon."

"Not long before I met you in the churchyard?"

He nodded. "I had just come from there; I was petrified."

Esther said, "Tell him what you saw earlier."

Edward ran his tongue over his lips. "I spent most of the day sketching around Druid's Rock, which is a couple of miles from Ruby's place, but I could see the cottage from where I was. About four o'clock or a bit later I started to pack up. I happened to glance across at the cottage and I saw smoke coming from the chimney."

"That surprised you?"

"Yes, it did. It was a hot day and Ruby only used a fire for heating; she did everything else by electricity."

"Go on."

"Well, I didn't think a lot about it but I looked over there once or twice and I saw that the smoke soon died away. Then I started out for home and when I was about a quarter of a mile from the cottage I saw someone come out of the garden door and walk off along the footpath towards the village."

"A man or a woman?"

"Oh, I'm sure it was a man though I couldn't see him well enough to recognize him."

"Can you describe what you did see?"

Edward frowned. "Well, I think he was fairly tall and he had dark trousers, I think, and a jacket or wind-cheater or something tight at the waist—that was dark too."

Years of interrogation had made Wycliffe acutely sensitive to changes in the manner of a witness—particularly when he or she stopped telling the truth and started to improvise. He felt sure that

Edward had done that now, though he was by no means sure where the improvisation had begun.

"Was there anything familiar about the man you saw?"

"No. Nothing!"

A mysterious stranger, in fact.

"You weren't close enough to describe him very clearly but you are able to say that he was like no one you know."

Edward flushed but said nothing.

"What did you do?"

"I didn't do anything. What could I do? I just walked on till I came to the cottage and let myself in by the garden door as usual. I didn't realize that there was anything wrong."

"Go on."

"Well, I went to the back door of the house, which was open, and I called out, "It's me!" There was no answer but I could hear loud music coming from upstairs. I knew that she was a bit deaf so I went up. . . . I looked in the room, and there she was. . . ." He swallowed hard, then added, "I could see the wound in her head; I knew she must be dead."

"Did you touch her?"

He shuddered and shook his head. Edward had not shaved and dark bristles stood out on his sallow skin so that with his hollow cheeks he looked almost corpse-like.

"I panicked. . . ."

There would have to be a formal interrogation so Wycliffe was content to let the boy tell his story. "When you visited Ruby, what did you talk about?"

"All sorts of things; she liked to hear anything and everything about the family and about Ashill."

"Did she resent the fact that she was not as welcome at Ashill as she had been in the past?"

He frowned. "Sometimes she said things which made me think she was upset about it."

"What sort of things?"

Edward hesitated and Wycliffe pressed him, "Ruby is dead— murdered, you say you didn't kill her. If we are to believe you, you will have to be completely truthful and frank."

"Well, she would say things like, 'They've a lot to thank me for but you'd never think so; I'm treated like a leper!' and 'It's a good thing I'm not one to bear a grudge.'"

"Did she know what had happened to your parents?"

"Of course! That was while Aunt Rosemary was still living and she told her everything."

"Did you mind her knowing?"

"No, she was always pleasant to me. In any case, I don't suppose it could have been very secret; it must have been in the newspapers at the time though I don't remember that."

"Do you think people in the village connected you with what they might have read in the newspapers about your parents?"

"No, I don't think they did—at least, not until recently. . . ."

"What happened recently?"

"I met Bunny Newcombe one afternoon when I was on my way back from the moor—about a fortnight ago, it was. Whenever I met him he used to look at me with a funny sort of grin; when I was young I used to be scared of him. Anyway, this time he said, 'Do you ever hear from your father? He must be out now, they only do a few years for a killing these days.'"

"Was that all?"

"Yes. I didn't say anything; I just walked on."

"*Do* you ever hear from your father?"

"No!"

Wycliffe was at a loss to guess at the relationship between Esther and the boy. It was as though, having arranged the interview, she sat in on it to make sure that her protégé performed properly.

During the questioning Wycliffe had got up from his seat and was moving about the room, looking at this and that, sometimes standing with his back to the room, staring out of the window at the beech trees on the other side of the Green. At one point he was near a batch of canvases, propped facing the wall. He stooped to pick one up. "May I look?"

Edward seemed tongue-tied and Esther said, "Edward doesn't like people looking at his work while he is there."

He had no reason or right to insist. He said, "You painted a picture for Ruby Price."

Edward looked embarrassed. "I painted the picture and she wanted to buy it so I gave it to her."

Wycliffe was standing with his hands behind his back, trying to decide on his next move. "You didn't hear the shot?"

"Shot?" Edward looked startled.

"The shot that killed her; probably the sound would carry across the open moor."

"I didn't hear anything."

Edward's position was too serious for anything but a formal approach. Wycliffe said, "I have to ask you to come to the police station at Newton to answer further questions and to make a formal statement. I will arrange for a car to pick you up at half past four. In the meantime you can take what advice you see fit."

Esther said, "Will he be allowed to leave again?"

"Certainly, if what he has told me is the whole truth."

Edward seemed to be relieved rather than otherwise.

Esther came with Wycliffe to see him off the premises. At the top of the steps she said to him, "Will he be in serious trouble for not saying that he found her earlier?"

"No. Failure to report a crime is antisocial but not criminal."

She stood, her hands resting on the rail, looking down at the cobbled yard and the old stables. She said, "Edward has a very rough time, you know; it's not only what happened when he was young, it's what happens now."

"What does happen?"

It was some time before she answered. "It's the way they treat him. . . . Aunt Naomi and Uncle Maurice treat him as though he was still a small boy and not very bright. . . . Uncle Nicholas ignores him completely but, of course, he ignores everyone these days. . . . Mostly it's my father and grandfather—they treat him as though he wasn't there most of the time; I mean, they don't even speak to him if he comes into the room, but if Grandfather does have anything to say it's always something cutting and hurtful."

"Why?"

She took time to think, then turned to him. "It's difficult to say why. To be 'in' with Grandfather you have to be exactly what he expects you to be. Edward doesn't come up to specification . . . not by a very long way."

"Do you?"

She treated the question very seriously. In fact, Wycliffe wondered if this girl ever laughed.

She said, "I could do very easily I went in for that sort of thing."

"Why does your father dislike Edward?"

A pause for thought. "He despises people who are not interested in money, and he can't use Edward for his own ends."

"That sounds very harsh."

"You asked the question."

She seemed reluctant to let him go and for the first time he sensed that her detachment, her serenity, might be no more than skin-deep.

He tried to leave on a lighter note. "I hope you are feeding the Newcombe livestock."

"Yes; it's no problem. I rather like doing it."

"Don't you have a job or something?"

"A job of sorts; I work mornings—Tuesdays to Saturdays—in a supermarket café in the city."

"Why not in the family firm with your father?"

She changed the subject. "Do you have children?"

"They're not children any more; they are older than you—twins, one of each."

"I suppose they have marvellous jobs." There was no trace of irony in her tone.

"I think they are both interested in what they do."

He was puzzled; she seemed in an uneasy, wistful mood. Suddenly she said, "We are talking as though we were both on the same side," and with that she left him and went indoors.

Wycliffe was in the little interview cubicle, staring out of the window at the action on the Green—volunteer labour, the men working twice as hard as they would have done for pay. He was brooding on the Beales; it had become almost a way of life for him. What did they *do?* That was not precisely the question he wanted to ask but it was as near as he could get. When Esther had finished playing at being a waitress in the supermarket café did she spend the rest of her time swanning around looking like something out of a Monet poppy field? Vicary—her father—was absorbed in his work, but Wycliffe did not believe in that mythical beast, the Computer Man. How did he unwind—blow off steam? Even Maurice must do something when he tired of the effort of trying to look like a high-powered executive. And Nicholas . . . Nicholas who looked like a man of destiny but had nowhere to go . . . Gertrude, an unknown quantity; Naomi, with her frustrations and spites barely held in check. . . . To say nothing of Simon, the ringmaster.

He could not remember a case in which he had been so out of contact with the people concerned; he felt an overwhelming need to *break in.*

"I've seen Billy Reynolds, sir." Sergeant Willis was standing in the doorway. Perhaps Wycliffe looked blank for he added, "The chap who used to work in Beales' D.I.Y. department."

Wycliffe nodded. "Come in."

Willis seemed to fill the little room with his bulk and his movements were self-consciously restrained. "He well remembers Vicary joining the firm, sir—he came there as a youngster—seventeen or eighteen, and he must have looked something like he does now for they christened him 'the Chimp' but it wasn't long before he showed what he was made of. Simon put him in charge of checking requisitions from the departments and making out order forms but inside six months Vicary had worked out an entirely new system of stock control which remained in use until they went over to computers in their new building."

Willis grinned. "I gather that the staff didn't care much for their whiz-kid but they had to admit he was something special."

"How about his marriage to the Beale girl?"

Willis made a wry face. "It came as a complete surprise to everybody. Vicary had been with the firm eight or nine years by then and was virtually in charge of accounts—"

"Was he living with his parents?"

"No; as soon as he was able to support himself he moved into a flat with a friend—no queer business, apparently—and the arrangement lasted for several years. After a while, Vicary found a girl he was keen on and was all set to marry, then Bingo! It was all off and in no time at all he was married to the Beale girl."

"Had she spent much time at the store?"

"Reynolds said he'd never seen her and neither had most of the staff."

"I don't suppose you know the name of Vicary's old flat-mate?"

"Reynolds did—it's Patterson; he did well for himself too, he's now a partner in Duxbury's—the Blue Chip Garage chain. Lives in Sutton Drive, and you can't do that on social security."

Wycliffe and Kersey spent two hours with Edward at the Newton police station during the latter part of which Maurice adopted dramatic postures in the waiting-room. The boy answered their questions without apparent resentment; pale and tense, but lucid and concise. It was obvious that Kersey was surprised and impressed.

One new fact emerged. Asked if he had ever fired a gun, Edward had replied: "Oh, yes. When I was a boy and Nicholas was on leave, he used to set up a target at the bottom of the garden. I didn't care a lot for it but he said it was up to everyone to prepare to defend the country against anarchy."

"What did you use, a sporting rifle?"

"Oh, no. We used his automatic; the one that's been stolen."

It was only much later that Wycliffe and Kersey were to look back and realize that if they had pursued this line of questioning a life might have been saved.

On one point only, Edward's story collapsed: "This man you saw leaving the cottage when you were on your way back from the moor . . ."

Wycliffe saw the deep flush rise from the boy's neck and suffuse his pale face. "There was no man, was there? You saw nobody, did you?"

He shook his head.

"Then why did you invent him?"

There was a longish silence before he answered, then he said, "I thought nobody would believe the truth. . . . I thought if I said I saw somebody leaving . . . I thought it would make it all more believable. . . ."

Wycliffe was home by a little after seven and he found Helen in the garden.

"There's a lamb casserole in the oven; an apricot crumble to follow, and I've put a bottle of Barsac in the fridge."

"What's this in aid of? I haven't forgotten an anniversary, have I?"

The garden was reaching its spring peak with magnolias, azaleas and rhododendrons competing for the eye. Through the shrubbery they could glimpse the waters of the estuary, scintillating in the sunlight. The gales and vicious driving rains of winter were forgotten.

"We are lucky." He was thinking of the Beales.

"Yes." She was thinking of the little back-to-back terraced house in which she had been brought up. She added, "I heard on the news about the second murder."

That accounted for the Barsac.

Helen had laid a table in the window of the living-room, overlooking the garden and the river beyond. They ate a leisurely meal; music by courtesy of M. Claude Debussy. Scrumptious!

Afterwards, while they were having their coffee, he became restless and in the end she said, "You'd better do it if you feel you must."

"Do what?"

"Whatever it is."

He looked up a number in the directory and telephoned. "Mr. Patterson?"

"Speaking."

"Chief Superintendent Wycliffe. I would like to come and see you this evening if possible."

"Can you tell me what it's about?" Wary, with a hint of apprehension.

"It's possible you may be able to help us with an inquiry we have on hand. You are not directly concerned."

"It all sounds very mysterious, Superintendent, but I always make a point of being accommodating to the police. Will ten o'clock suit you? Or is that too late?"

"No, ten o'clock suits me."

"It's the top flat; there is a speak-box in the entrance hall."

Sutton Drive, overlooking the sea, was one of the most prestigious residential areas in the city; a terrace of tall, mid-Victorian houses, covered with white stucco and looking like a gigantic wedding-cake. Built for wealthy Victorian families with no servant problem, they were five storeys high; now they had been furnished with lifts and split up into luxury flats.

Patterson was sturdily built and fair, his tendency to baldness not entirely hidden by a toupee, and he had that carefully groomed, well-preserved look of an ageing bachelor fighting a rearguard action against time.

Wycliffe was shown into a large sitting-room at the very top of the house; the curtains were drawn back and the window looked out to a vast expanse of sea, silvery in the darkness. Erotic Beardsley prints in stainless steel frames hung on white walls; there were a whitish carpet and club-chairs covered with white leather. It was obvious that Patterson provided a temporary roost for any birds of passage who happened along.

Wycliffe got straight to business: "My inquiries concern the Washford murders. You will understand that we have to cast our net wide and I hope you won't read too much into my questions which are purely—"

"Routine." Patterson finished for him.

It was a relief occasionally to deal with someone who habitually sails sufficiently near the wind to know the ropes.

"How can I help you?"

"A number of years ago you shared a flat with Frank Vicary who is now a director of Beales' Household Stores—"

"And married to the boss's daughter." Patterson grinned. "So that's it! I hardly think I shall be able to tell you much, I haven't seen Frankie above twice in twenty years."

"You quarrelled?"

A canny look. "No. After sharing a flat with him for five years he walked out on me at less than a week's notice; that's all."

"He left to get married."

Patterson was sitting, self-consciously nonchalant, in one of his club-chairs. "As you say, he left to get married."

"You must have known it was in the offing, surely?"

"I don't think he knew himself."

"But he must have been seeing the girl; perhaps you didn't share in his social life?"

Wycliffe received a knowing grin. "We didn't have a scintillating social life; a beer at the local and a couple of girls on lucky weekends was the outside of it. Believe it or not, we were two hard-working guys from pretty dreary backgrounds, determined to beat the system. We worked at our jobs all day and did evening classes and correspondence courses in our spare time. Accountancy, law, business admin and God knows what else. In the end, Frankie got hooked on a girl. She was a pleasant, homely sort of kid, just waiting to turn herself into a good wife and mother. I don't think he was leading her up the garden; he used to talk to me quite seriously about when they were married though he wasn't in a rush to sign her up. Then, from one day to the next, it was all off; Frankie was to marry the Beale chick."

Patterson turned to face Wycliffe. "Lucky—that was the kid's name—was absolutely floored; I don't know what happened to the poor little bastard but I've never seen anybody so winded. It was bloody cruel."

"Had he ever mentioned the Beale girl before?"

"Never!"

"They had a child seven months later."

"So I've heard. All I can say, if Frankie seduced his boss's daughter he must have done it in the firm's time. I must admit I was staggered. After all, he wasn't exactly a sex symbol and she, according to all accounts, was a poppet."

"You've no idea what actually happened?"

Patterson frowned. "My guess is there was some sort of deal but why, in the name of God? I mean, what did the Beales get out of it? I know Frankie is a damned good accountant but you don't have to trade in your daughter for a good accountant."

Patterson broke off and glanced at the gilded sun-ray clock above the fireplace. "I don't want to be inhospitable but I'm expecting a guest. . . ."

Wycliffe felt fairly sure he had got all he was likely to—probably all Patterson had to give—so he got up to go. As he was leaving a blond girl in a low-cut dress and a fur stole got out of the lift. Patterson was hovering and winked when he caught Wycliffe's eye.

Wycliffe came away feeling that he now had most of the pieces but not the least idea how to put them together. Experience had taught him not to try too hard. Over the hours and days ahead words and phrases recalled; faces and episodes vividly remembered, would present themselves to his mind; patterns would suggest themselves only to be examined and rejected. . . . But what if there was another crime?

He drove through the empty city streets, out into the country on the other side, through the lanes which would bring him to the watch house. For the last mile he could look down on the estuary, shining dimly. A sizeable merchant ship in ballast was slipping downstream with the tide, her superstructure picked out in lights. Sometimes he fancied himself a skipper on the bridge of such a ship, on her way down-channel, bound for Bombay or Colombo; Lagos or Rio. . . . He yawned, and the car swerved. Captain MacWhirr was tired.

Helen was in the drawing-room, watching television; the curtains were not drawn and he could still see the lights of his ship as she gathered speed beyond the narrows.

Chapter Five

Another fine day: the air had a gentle freshness, and the light a glowing quality which belongs to a fine morning in an English spring. But in his office, where it was impossible to open a window and the air was "conditioned" the atmosphere, as usual, was second-hand, limp and apathetic, as flat beer.

"But who am I to be cheerful?"—Wycliffe facing the fact that he had two murders on his hands and was no nearer a solution.

Franks had sent in his preliminary report on the Ruby Price post-mortem but the only significant passage referred to the time of death: ". . . some time on Monday, April 27th. It is difficult to support a more precise estimate with firm evidence but my impression is that death probably occurred after midday and before midnight. . . ."

This was consistent with Edward's story but it also underlined his vulnerability, for, if Franks was right, Edward had been with the dead woman within a short time of her death.

The routine of the day got under way; he signed forms, dealt with queries, dictated letters and memoranda until a few minutes before half-past ten so that even Diane was satisfied.

"Now you've got a press briefing; it's in the car-park for the benefit of the TV people. You've also got a note in the diary of Newcombe's funeral—three o'clock this afternoon, from the Fretwells'."

Already these names were commonplace in the office, names of people whom Diane had never seen, and never even heard of three days earlier.

The press and television were making up for previous indifference and there was an impressive gathering on the car-park.

"The man you detained last night, Mr. Wycliffe—"

"No one was detained. Mr. Edward Beale cooperated with us and made a statement about his visits to the dead woman."

"Isn't it true that he discovered the body?"

"Yes, that is so."

"And failed to report it?"

"Mr. Beale told me of his discovery yesterday afternoon."

"Forty-eight hours after the event?"

"That is correct."

"Are you any nearer an arrest following the interrogation of this young man?"

"No."

"Is it the case that the weapon which killed Newcombe and the woman, Price, was the property of Captain Nicholas Beale of Ashill?"

"It is true that an automatic pistol belonging to Captain Beale is missing; it is also true that our ballistics expert considers that the bullet which killed Mr. Newcombe was fired from such a pistol. As yet I have had no report on this aspect of the second killing."

"Do you think that the villagers have reason to fear further outrages?"

"I can't answer that; all I can say is that our patrols should help to reassure them."

"Are you aware of uneasiness among the villagers concerning alleged reluctance on the part of the police to follow certain leads?"

"I can well understand that the villagers are uneasy. As to leads, we shall continue to investigate fully every suspicious circumstance which comes to our notice."

"Are you looking for a madman or for someone with a real grievance against his victims?"

"I have no information about the murderer's state of mind."

And so on. The usual charade by which reporters fulfil their sacred duty and some harassed official tries to avoid saying something which could boomerang.

By midday Wycliffe was back in Washford; in the upper room which had shared Ruby's heart with her garden. Three men were at work there; a young man from Forensic was sorting through a quantity of half-burnt paper and even trying to make something of the ash itself. Real Sherlock Holmes stuff this, with forceps and lens. The contents of several of Ruby's envelopes had been reduced to ash or had survived only as charred remains.

The second man in the room was D.C. Fowler, the oldest member of Wycliffe's squad. He could be relied upon to work away at the most boring job without pause and without complaint but he was by no means stupid. Now, with glasses on the end of his nose, he was going through the contents of Ruby's other envelopes, those which had not been damaged.

Each envelope had a name on it—the name of one of her "babies" and in it was stored, on odd scraps of paper, every bit of information she had been able to gather. All was grist to Ruby's mill, from the winning of a school prize or an attack of measles, to details of love affairs, marriage, job problems, parenthood and, in a few cases, death. It was all there, each envelope a data-bank for a biography and an intimate one at that.

Fowler said, "Some of this would come in handy to an enterprising village blackmailer—or a poison pen."

Was that the explanation of her murder? Was she a blackmailer or, more credibly, a poison-pen writer? If so, where did Newcombe come in? It was hard to imagine them working as a team.

Fowler went on, "As far as I can see, there's nothing on the Beales."

Which might mean that Ruby saw the family as out of her range, or it could mean that what concerned the Beales was now part of the charred paper and ash being studied by the boffin from Forensic.

The third man, completing the research team, was new to the squad—a dyed-in-the-wool Cornishman called Curnow, a young man of deceptively gentle speech and manner. He was going through Ruby's diaries—half a dozen hard-covered exercise books in which she had noted down a terse record of her days.

"It's not much of a diary, sir, more a list of things she did and of people she visited; when she planted her seeds or bottled her wine or cut back her raspberries. I started with the current book and I'm working back but there's one recent entry you might want to see."

Curnow handed him the book and pointed to the entry. Written in Ruby's round, schoolgirl hand, it was dated a month earlier, and it read: "Honoured by a visit from Nicky—the first since dear R died. He took an hour to come to the point which was that he has found romance—or thinks he has. He is worried that it might be blighted if the lady found out certain things. Her name wasn't mentioned but I've known about it for some time. Poor Nicky! I wonder what R would have made of it?"

For some reason Wycliffe called to mind the well-trodden path through the woods between Ashill and Quarry House about which the forthright Veronica had seemed oddly self-conscious. The idea of the ponderous and repressed Nicky having found romance at forty-six had its ludicrous side, but also a certain pathos, but had it anything to do with the case?

Routine. That blessed word. The uncomfortable truth was that he hadn't the least idea what to do next except plough on with the business of collecting information and hoping that significant correlations would emerge. It was orthodox procedure and though he was wary of a surfeit of facts he had to toe the line; in these days a policeman works with one eye on the press and politicians.

Depressed, he went downstairs.

The whole house and garden had been turned upside down and men were tramping around the village again with their ball-points and clipboards. Statements were being taken, typed, photo-copied, and filed. God alone knew how many people were involved. . . . And the murderer—what was he doing? A question of more than academic interest. A pathological killer would be at a certain stage of his traumatic cycle; he had achieved release but the initial euphoria would be followed first, by a sense of anticlimax, perhaps a wave of self-disgust, then the germ of a new desire, the growth of a fresh appetite. . . . One feature among others which made Wycliffe sceptical of the psychopath notion was the proximity in time of the two crimes; it was not conclusive but it was suggestive.

But if the killer was a "rational" being with a credible motive, what would he be doing? It would presumably depend on how far his objective had been achieved. Either way it was a question of two down; how many to go?

He walked along Vicarage Road and down North Street; the sun shone out of a clear blue sky and flags were strung across the street between the houses. Some of the flags were of real bunting, faded and bleached by the celebrations of a century. The murders had not been allowed to cast any blight on the preparations and the whole village wore a cheerful, almost a carnival aspect. On the Green, near the platform, men were erecting a tall and colourful maypole.

Wycliffe went into the pub for a snack lunch and was surprised to find a good crowd of locals as well as men from the fair: the locals wore their best clothes and there was a holiday atmosphere, a good-tempered rowdiness with plenty of laughs. But as Wycliffe approached the bar they fell silent and all eyes turned on him.

The landlord greeted him with an air of amused tolerance. "Well, sir, what can we do for you?" He pointed to the chalkboard. "As you see, we've got a bit more on offer today."

He ordered beer and a helping of cottage pie. The landlord repeated his order in a loud voice to an invisible Dora and turned back to him.

"Shall we be seeing you at the fair tomorrow, sir?"

"I hope so."

"No arrest yet?"

"No."

The whole room was listening; even the men from the fair had stopped talking among themselves, realizing that something was up. Dora, red-faced from bending over a hot stove, brought his pie on a heated plate, with a knife and fork wrapped in a paper napkin. He took it with his beer to a vacant place near one of the windows but the hubbub which had greeted him was not resumed. It was as though they waited for a cue and the cue was not long in coming.

Wycliffe had noticed the little red-headed shopkeeper, Chas. Alford, at the centre of a small group of men who were plying him with drinks. In the group was another of the tradesmen Wycliffe recognized, the tobacconist and confectioner, Sam Brimblecombe, a stout, florid man who seemed to live with a short-stemmed pipe between his teeth.

Alford cleared his throat and said in a loud cawing voice, intended for the whole company, "They had young Beale at the nick in Newton last night; kept him there for two hours."

All eyes now turned on the redhead.

Alford went on, "I reckon they don't pull in a chap with his connections unless they got very good reason, but after two hours they let'n go."

Another of the group, an obvious "feed," enquired, "Why would they do that, do you think, Charlie?"

A knowing smile. "Well, you'd hardly expect me to be what you might call 'in' with the police, but I do know something about the way these things work—the way they're *worked.*" He paused, then went on, "My guess is, Uncle Simon phoned his friend, the chief constable."

There was an uneasy laugh and several eyes turned on the superintendent, who went on with his meal, apparently oblivious.

But the redhead had not finished. "Laugh if you like, but what if there's another killing tonight? That wouldn't be very funny, would it? Another innocent man or woman with a bullet through the head. Not funny at all!"

Wycliffe happened to glance across at the landlord and caught the old man watching him with an amused expression. Blatchford was enjoying himself.

Alford went on, "I believe in looking at a man's *stock,* just like with a horse or a bullock. My father used to say, 'Bad blood will out'—"

"And he should know all about that, Charlie!" A voice from another part of the room which Alford ignored.

"That's not fashionable these days but there's a lot of things that aren't fashionable but is still true. Take this young man we're speaking of, for instance; one or two of us just happen to know his father was sentenced to 'life' for murdering his wife. Now, the police know all about that—they should—and if I was they, I'd think about that; I'd think a lot about it. And all we ought to think about it too."

There was a murmur of approval which sounded genuine.

Encouraged, the little redhead went on: "But there's more to it than that. You can't just say, 'Like father, like son'; you got to have evidence. That's only right. Well, this young man we're talking about, says he found Ruby Price, lying dead—shot through the head —a woman we all thought well of, who done a tremendous amount of good for the village and brought most of us into this world. This young man, a regular visitor of Ruby's, found her shot, *but he didn't tell anybody.*"

An impressed silence.

"He didn't tell anybody for two days and then only when the police come to question him. Now, we got to ask ourselves, *why* didn't he tell anybody? Why?"

Another pause for dramatic effect but this time it was fatal. A wag spoke up: "I expect 'e forgot. After all, Charlie, you forget some things—like paying yer bills an' doing yer flies up when there's young girls about."

There was a great burst of laughter and the little redhead tried to hide his confusion by pretending he had dropped something on the floor. It was not long before conversation returned to normal and then numbers began to thin.

As he was leaving, Wycliffe said to the landlord, "Charlie Alford —is he the voice of the village?"

"He'd like to think so."

"They're not taken in?"

Blatchford grinned. "What do you think?"

"That there was some stage-management."

Blatchford's grin turned to a chuckle. "They're a bit like school-boys—mischievous; and all the excitement's gone to their heads. Now they've got Bunny's funeral this afternoon and the fair to-morrow."

"Will many of them be at the funeral?"

"All of 'em! Why do you think they're off work and all dressed up?"

As Wycliffe was turning away the landlord added, "All the same, sir, don't get it wrong; there's plenty of genuine feeling."

The procession assembled at the top of North Street, outside the Fretwells', with more than a hundred men walking behind the hearse and a single car for the principal mourners. The coffin was smothered in flowers; more were piled on the hearse and on the roof of the following car. Wycliffe found himself walking next to the innkeeper, who had obviously contrived it. Blatchford, his red face contrasting with his white halo of hair, bulged out of a dark pin-stripe suit.

"So Jimmy kept it in the family."

"Jimmy?"

"Fretwell; that's his hearse, his car and his men driving. It don't seem right to bury your own relative; I thought he would've got a trade price from old Martin the undertaker over to Shotleigh, but trust a Fretwell not to spend a penny if a ha'penny will do."

The funeral procession seemed out of place under the strings of flags but it was obvious that none of the villagers saw anything incongruous about it; an occasion was an occasion and whether it was sad or gay made little difference. It had been the same in his own village.

The women were at their windows, peering between the curtains which were nominally drawn. The shops were shut and there was no one in the street.

Blatchford said, "In any other circumstances most of 'em would be saying: 'A damn good riddance!' "

Wycliffe wondered what the scruffy little fat man himself would have made of it all.

As they approached the Green, Blatchford said, "You must've wondered a bit about Charlie Alford. Charlie's got it in for the Beales; he worked in their Newton branch and got the sack for interfering with a girl cashier. After that he set up on his own with money borrowed from his wife's family but he's never made a go of it, he's in debt everywhere and people wonder how he can carry on." All this *sotto voce* so that his words would not reach the men walking in front or behind. "Charlie's got a chip on his shoulder the size of a plank."

They filed into the church, where there was a short service, then they moved to the graveside, with the mourners spreading out over the adjoining graves and paths. The great majority of the men were unknown to Wycliffe. He assumed that the rather pompous fat man, who seemed to be chief mourner, must be Martha's husband—the undertaker himself. Simon was there, standing bare-headed and alone, like a patriarch; and Wycliffe saw Dr. Sharpe, looking ominously flushed, constantly fingering his moustache. He caught sight of little Alford and their eyes met for an instant, but Alford looked away quickly. Brimblecombe from the sweet-shop, for once without his pipe, stood by a very tall, bony man whom Wycliffe knew to be the butcher from the shop on the Green.

When it was over and Wycliffe was leaving the churchyard, still in company with the innkeeper, he said, "It's time we had a serious talk—without an audience."

Blatchford turned to look at him. "I've been thinking so myself; come back with me, Mr. Wycliffe, and have a little something."

They crossed the Green under the strings of flags and coloured lamps. The men of the village were gathering in groups, reluctant to break up and go home. But for the licensing laws there would have been no dilemma. Everybody had a word for the innkeeper and Wycliffe sensed that his own stock had risen through being seen in Blatchford's company.

They went into the inn by the back door, through the overwarm kitchen where Dora was brushing milk onto rows of pasties and pies laid out on sheaths, ready for the oven.

"Getting ready for tomorrow," Blatchford said, "She's got a freezer full of stuff already."

"Somebody's got to do it," Dora said.

Wycliffe was taken into the parlour which overlooked the vegetable garden and the backs of houses in South Street.

"Sit you down, Mr. Wycliffe. Light up if you want to; I know you're a pipe smoker. Do you like scrumpy?"

Wycliffe was not partial to the local rough cider which gave him an acid stomach and a heavy hangover, but he wanted to fall in with the innkeeper's mood.

The old man was all smiles, a little unsure of himself. "Back in a minute." He lumbered out of the room and returned with an earthenware jug of cider and two tankards. "There we are! All nice and cool, straight from the wood."

Wycliffe was still standing, looking at a large framed photograph of a young woman with small but strong features and a nineteen-thirties hair-style.

Blatchford said, "Sarah—my wife. She's been dead ten years come Whitsun."

"I can see the resemblance."

"Resemblance?"

"To Joyce at Ashill—weren't they sisters?"

The old man grinned. "You've been finding out about us, sir!"

The preliminaries had taken three or four minutes by the pendulum wall-clock which had a prancing horse on the top. Now Blatchford settled his great body into a wing-chair and placed the jug of cider on a table close to his hand.

"Right, Mr. Wycliffe."

Wycliffe said, "Did your wife get on well with her sister?"

Mild surprise; obviously not the sort of question the innkeeper had expected. "Get on? They was very close; their parents died young and I think that makes for closeness between the children—"

"And I suppose Emily Newcombe must have been on friendly terms with them both—I mean, working all those years at Ashill with Joyce."

Blatchford was puzzled. "They was very friendly, as you say, but—"

"So that one way and another not much could go on at Ashill that you didn't hear about."

The old man looked put out. "I know you think I've been holding back, Mr. Wycliffe, that's because I don't gossip; a publican's got to be careful—can't afford to let his tongue run away with him—but I can tell you this, sir, if I knew anything about these murders you would hear it soon enough. As to the Beales, whatever my wife thought, I never had a great opinion of the family." He took a good gulp of cider, then wiped his lips with a handkerchief the size of a small table-cloth. "All the same, I got to admit there's something that's been on my mind a bit." He fixed Wycliffe with clear candid blue eyes.

"When you was in my bar on Monday you mentioned about Emily having some money laid by and I put you off—I said it was only a yarn, a sort of village joke. Well, since then I've been thinking that maybe there was a bit more to it; in fact, you put me in mind of something Sarah told me"—he glanced up at his wife's photograph —"Sarah had a head for business, which is more than I ever did, and Joyce and Emily used to come to her whenever they had any little problems in the way of business—not that they had many! Anyway, I mind Sarah telling me that Emily was asking her about how to invest a sum of money so that it would be safe."

The old man chuckled. "Wouldn't we all like to know the answer to that, sir? Well, you could buy gold then, just like you can now if you got the money, and I remember Sarah said she'd told Emily to buy sovereigns. Sarah had put a bit of her own money in gold about then. Of course, I've no idea whether Emily took her advice."

"When was this?"

Blatchford shook his head. "I couldn't put a date on it, Mr. Wycliffe, but it must've been in the early sixties. I know it was several years after Emily lost her husband."

"Any idea of the sum involved?"

Another shake of the head. "No, but Sarah did say she thought it was a fairish amount—enough to make her wonder where it came from, if you understand me, sir."

"And did she or you find out?"

A shrewd grin. "No, we didn't, but I will say this, Mr. Wycliffe, people in this village don't part with their money without getting value for it."

"What does that mean?"

Blatchford looked innocently vague. "Mean? I don't know what it means, sir; it's just a fact."

Wycliffe was feeling the first effects of the cider he had drunk, a certain mellowness, a sense of relaxed well-being. Blatchford sat bolt upright in his chair; with his bulk he could hardly do otherwise; one large, freckled hand grasped his tankard, the other held on to the arm of the chair. "Let me top you up, Mr. Wycliffe . . . there's plenty more where that came from."

They were silent for a while. The fair had started up and they could hear the music from across the Green.

When Blatchford spoke again it was in a mood of reminiscence. "It's hard to believe Bunny's gone. . . . Odd sort of chap. He wasn't very bright; I don't think he ever learned to read and write properly but he had a sort of cunning. . . ." A deep sigh and a draught of cider. "And he was clever with animals! I've never seen anything like it. You should've seen him with a little wire-haired terrier bitch he had—talk about tricks!

"And birds—he could charm the birds out of the trees; they'd come and feed out of his hand—out of his mouth!" A chuckle that shook his whole body. "Animals, birds and women—you'd never believe to see him latterly that, as a youngster, he was a fairish-looking chap. The girls used to think so anyway—he never had any problem in that direction. He'd have the pants off 'em before they could remember what it was Mother had told 'em. Then there was a bit of bother about some under-age little piece over to Biscombe and from then on Emily did her best to put a stop to his games." A broad grin. "I reckon she had her work cut out!

"The funny thing was he never made any friends; there was only one chap he was ever at all matey with and that was Charlie Alford. Bunny used to buy the few bits and pieces he needed for his odd jobs from Charlie's shop."

The innkeeper sighed once more. "As I say, Bunny wasn't the brightest but he must've had something; he didn't get shot for nothing and neither did poor old Ruby." The blue eyes were devoid of any expression. "It must all tie up, sir, but I'm blowed if I can see how."

Wycliffe changed the subject. "Was it generally known in the village that young Edward's father had murdered his mother?"

Blatchford frowned. "No, it wasn't. Simon's wife's family were sort of outsiders and nobody knew much about 'em."

"Yet Alford knew."

"Yes, he did; and he made sure to spread it around but that was recent; how and when he found out I couldn't tell you, sir."

"Thanks for the cider." Wycliffe got up to go and Blatchford made no attempt to dissuade him but came with him to the door.

"I hope I haven't wasted your time, sir."

It was Wycliffe's turn to be enigmatic: "We shall see, shan't we?"

The sunshine took him by surprise after the dimly lit parlour, so did the atmosphere of liveliness around the Green. The men had finally gone home after the funeral and it was the turn of the women with young children; they were trailing across the Green to the fairground, giving the youngsters a treat before bed.

Wycliffe crossed the Green to the police van, wondering what to make of the old humbug's erratic powers of recall and more than half convinced that he had said nothing without some definite purpose.

Decoded, Blatchford's message seemed to be that in the early sixties the Beales had presented Emily Newcombe with a substantial sum of money; that Bunny had been, in his younger days, a bucolic Don Juan; and that Charlie Alford might be worth a second look.

In the van Kersey was waiting for him with the man from forensic who, because of his outsize ears, Kersey had christened Dumbo. Dumbo was anxious to get back to his laboratory to work on some of the material and he promised to send his report as soon as possible.

Wycliffe's reaction probably seemed less than enthusiastic; he doubted whether the case would now be solved by anything out of Ruby's envelopes and the cider he had drunk was making him drowsy. When the man from forensic had gone Wycliffe said, "Anything else?"

Kersey yawned. The sun streamed in through one of the little windows and it was very warm. He turned the pages of his notes. "Fowler has gone back to write his report on the unburnt stuff in the envelopes but he gave me the gist of what he found. Nothing directly relevant but plenty of material for a blackmailer. There's no doubt Ruby knew all about life in the village, including the seamy side. At first you'd get the impression the place was a sort of Sodom but when you weigh it up it's probably no better and no worse than anywhere else. A few kids call the wrong bloke "daddy" and some of 'em have been doing it long enough to have kids of their own. One family seems to specialize in incest as a sort of tradition; the chap who runs the paint shop—Alford—goes around showing himself to young girls, and the butcher, according to his wife, has one or two novel sexual habits. . . ."

Kersey sighed. "Ruby must have been a remarkable old girl—they *told* her these things and she wrote them all down. You'd think she was doing a Kinsey on Washford and yet, according to Franks, she herself died a virgin."

Wycliffe said, "Some people prefer to live by proxy—it's safer. But speaking of Alford, I've a suspicion it was Alford who sent the anonymous note. Get somebody sensible to talk to him. According to Blatchford he was fairly close to Newcombe so there could be something there. They'll have to lean on him a bit."

Kersey said, "There's one other thing in the reports. The milk-man, Hext, says he saw Newcombe coming away from Ruby's place on Thursday morning. Newcombe was coming out of Ruby's gate, muttering to himself; Hext asked him what was up and Newcombe said: 'That bloody old cow in there; that's what's up!' "

Wycliffe said, "The register office on Wednesday afternoon and the midwife on Thursday morning, it ought to mean something."

"But what could he have hoped to find out?"

"Whatever it was, it seems Ruby sent him going with a flea in his ear."

Kersey stretched his arms high above his head and yawned once more. "Now they're both dead; it doesn't make sense."

Wycliffe said, "Nicholas went to see Ruby, and he's not dead."

Gertrude Vicary dozed in an armchair in the drawing-room of her flat on the first floor at Ashill. She had kicked off her shoes and her stockinged feet were tucked under her body. A low sun flooded the room with light, blinding the television set on which a chat-show was in full cry. Jumbled music from the fairground reached into the room, muted but insistent.

Esther came in; she stood for a moment, gazing down at her mother, then she went to the television and switched it off. The mantel-clock chimed; a quarter to seven. Gertrude stirred.

"Oh, it's you." She glanced at the clock. "God! I must have been asleep; your father will be here soon." She stood up, stepped into her shoes, settled her hair and smoothed her frock. She tried to cover a certain confusion with words.

"Have you just come in? Where have you been?"

"I told you I wasn't going out this afternoon."

"So you did; I'd forgotten."

A door opened and closed; footsteps in the hall. Although the flat had its own separate entrance and stairs, on his arrival home each evening Vicary always called on his father-in-law, then he would enter the flat through the communicating door.

Gertrude stood still, an odd little smile on her lips. "There he is . . . brief-case in study, glance at the post but don't open . . . cross hall to loo . . . pee . . . wash hands, comb through hair . . . examine features in glass, grimace, displaying own teeth . . . cross hall to drawing-room, "Oh, there you are!" She broke off with a puzzled look when the door did not open. "God! Something must have jammed the works!"

Esther was watching her mother. "You do hate him, don't you?"

Gertrude suddenly looked scared. "Of course I don't hate your father! Don't be absurd! I was joking."

At that moment the door did open and Vicary came in. "Ah! There you are!" He glanced round the room, taking everything in, just as he did when visiting one of the firm's depots, then he went over to his wife and placed a formal kiss on her forehead. It was almost a ritual gesture, as though after an absence, he felt the need to re-establish possession.

"Your father stopped me on the way up; the police are with Nicky at the moment."

Gertrude became very still. "Nicky! Why him, for God's sake?"

Vicary seemed to contemplate her concern. "I have no idea, but your father is very worried." He allowed this to sink in. "Of course, it was Nicky's gun and the police are very simple-minded. When you were questioned about the missing pistol, what happened?"

Gertrude frowned. "What happened? Nothing. . . . A young policeman came up here and wrote down my silly answers to his stupid questions."

"Did you refer to Nicky's past at all?"

"His past? You mean the army business? Of course not!"

Vicary acknowledged his daughter for the first time and said curtly, "And you, Esther? You were questioned, I think."

Esther said in a flat voice, entirely devoid of expression, "I was questioned but I had nothing to tell them."

"You knew about your uncle's rather tragic experience."

"I knew about it but it had nothing to do with them or with the missing gun."

Vicary said, "I'm very glad you had the sense to see that." He added after a pause, "In that case they are probably badgering Nicky because they don't know what else to do!" His eyes returned to his wife; coldly possessive. "The old man is really rattled; I think we should all three go down to dinner tonight—a gesture."

Gertrude said, "Yes, let's make a gesture, by all means."

"Don't laugh at me, Gertrude."

"Laugh? What is there to laugh at? Edward was taken to the police station last night; Nicky is being interrogated tonight—I wonder when it will be my turn—or yours."

He continued to look at her but said nothing.

She became irritable under his eyes and snapped, "For God's sake don't watch me like that, Frank. . . . I haven't been drinking but I shall start at any minute if you go on like this!"

Esther watched her parents with that same quiet gaze with which one watches fish in an aquarium tank.

"I have nothing to say."

Nicholas had used these words two or three times already in response to certain questions. Wycliffe would have preferred the interview to take place in the more formal setting of an interview room at the police station but he did not want press reports of a second man "helping the police with their inquiries" and being allowed to go home afterwards. So Nicholas was facing him and Kersey on his home ground, surrounded by the reconstructed war games of Wellington and Soult, Massena and Beresford.

Kersey was speaking. "On April tenth you visited Ruby Price at her home and you told her of your association with a lady, not named. You asked Miss Price for a certain assurance—what was that assurance?"

"I have nothing to say."

"Did she give it you?"

"I have told you; I have nothing to say."

Nicholas sat motionless in his chair, behind the big desk, his eyes apparently focused on the opposite wall.

Wycliffe intervened. "You realize that your refusal to cooperate might lead us to think that you had a motive for killing Ruby Price?"

"That is nonsense!"

"Did you visit her on the day she died?"

"No; my only visit was about three weeks ago—you say it was the tenth."

"She was shot sometime on Monday afternoon."

"So?"

"Where were you at that time? You will remember that when Mr. Kersey called you were out, but you came in while he was here."

"I went for a walk as I often do after lunch."

"Who is the lady you talked about to Ruby Price?"

Nicholas did not answer and Wycliffe went on, "Is it one of the Gould sisters?"

Still no reply.

"It would be a simple matter to ask them."

It worked. Nicholas looked as though the possibility had not occurred to him. "That would be an abominable thing to do!"

"Which sister?"

"Miss Veronica." He spoke the name in that special way a boy speaks the name of his first girl. "I hope that you won't—"

"We shan't interfere in any way with your private life if you are frank with us, Captain Beale. Now will you tell us why you went to see Ruby Price?"

He shook his head. "I'm sorry; I can only tell you that it had nothing whatever to do with her death."

Wycliffe tried a different approach. "We are investigating two murders and it seems that they must be linked. Newcombe and Ruby Price were shot with an automatic pistol of nine-millimetre calibre—presumably yours. Can you suggest any connection between the two victims which might help to establish the motive?"

"I know of no connection; I find it hard to believe that there was one."

"We know that your brother-in-law visited Newcombe on the afternoon of the Sunday he was killed, to discuss arrangements about a pension paid—"

There was a sudden change in Nicholas; he flushed and said in a brittle voice, "I know nothing of my brother-in-law's activities. If his job was to conclude an arrangement with Newcombe I have no doubt that he was successful—he is good at that sort of thing, that is why my father makes use of him."

The contempt was blistering.

The questions continued but the answers, when they came, were not enlightening. It was gone seven when they left Ashill.

Kersey said, "He's no fool. Except on the subject of his brother-in-law he gave nothing away that he wasn't forced to. But talk about family solidarity! It seems possible he had some sort of motive for the Price killing; perhaps we should have turned the screw a bit more to find out what it was he's so anxious to keep from his girl-friend."

"He wouldn't have told us; he's obstinate on principle; the stuff martyrs are made of. It's probably connected in some way with his discharge from the army—a matter of honour. Nicky is strong on honour."

The fair was doing good business; the whole village seemed to be out and about, streaming across the Green to the field; children dragged along by their parents; young couples, arm in arm; raucous youths, aggressively playful, like young steers; groups of giggling girls sending out provocative signals. . . . The weather was idyllic; the evening sun still shone and the beeches around the Green cast long shadows.

In the van, Wycliffe slumped into a chair and stretched his legs as far as the chicken-coop accommodation allowed. He yawned, assailed by a great wave of tiredness.

He said, "Motive, means and opportunity. How many times have we heard that? Well, motive has got us nowhere yet. Means presents no problems: any one of the family—including Nicky of course—could have got hold of the gun. So let's look at opportunity."

Kersey reached down a file and turned the pages.

"Well, you know already that any one of them could have done the Newcombe killing. Between ten-fifteen and eleven-thirty on Sunday evening, no two of them were together. For a close-knit family they don't seem fond of each other's company."

"And Ruby Price?"

Kersey frowned. "That's a different story; it's difficult to get a clear picture. According to Franks, Ruby died on Monday afternoon

—that's as near as he's prepared to go and it lets all of 'em in, except Maurice, who was in his office as usual, trying to look like a business tycoon. Vicary spent the morning in Newton about a building contract; he had lunch at the Moorview in Bickington and in the afternoon he was at Tor Vale but we can't tie down the times anything like tight enough to let him out. Choosing his route he might easily have passed near Ruby's place without coming into Washford and without losing much time. He could have had an hour at the cottage for all we know."

"And Nicholas?"

Kersey turned a page. "Nicky says he went for a walk but as far as he can remember, he didn't meet anybody. Simon and Gertrude say they didn't leave the house, neither did Naomi, who was 'resting.' Monday is Esther's day off because the supermarket doesn't open and she says, after feeding Newcombe's livestock—we checked on that with our chaps there—she returned to the house and spent the rest of the afternoon reading in her room."

Wycliffe sighed. "That leaves Edward, who was on the moor, a sitting duck."

Chapter Six

May morning: a morning of misty sunshine with the promise of a fine warm day to come. Each house had a leafy branch of "may" secured to the front door and even if these had not been gathered by virgins in the small hours, at least they were there. As to virgins, those who, by reason of their tender age might be presumed so, were gathered on the Green, dressed in white frocks with green sashes, dancing round the maypole to the music of an accordion. A small crowd of parents, relatives and friends looked on. The coloured ribbons attached to the pole and held by the girls wound round the pole and unwound again as the dancers reversed their steps. The children's voices piped loud and clear:

> "Little May Rose turn round three times,
> Let us look at you round and round!"

Ten o'clock; the fair people were having their breakfasts; their children sat on the steps of the caravans and their dogs explored the site sniffing unfamiliar scents. The old men of the village, tricked out in their best suits, hung about in small groups, a little at a loose end; but everywhere in the beflagged streets there was an air of cheerful expectancy. The shops, due to close at eleven, were busy and their doorbells pinged incessantly.

Another police caravan was being moved in beside the first to provide a base for the additional men to be deployed during the fair. Wycliffe had made the arrangements with the uniformed branch; their men would mingle with the crowds, showing the flag, while patrol cars covered the outskirts, keeping an eye on isolated houses and farms. This was mainly a public relations exercise but he thought the villagers deserved some visible evidence of police concern.

But Wycliffe saw and heard all that was going on as one sees and hears a television programme when preoccupied with something else. During a restless night, when it seemed to him that he had scarcely lost consciousness for more than a few minutes, odd phrases had repeated themselves in his mind like one of those irritating jingles which refuse to be forgotten. Now, in the full light of day, he realized that he had been striving to marshal the facts and discern some sort of pattern.

He was still trying.

Newcombe at the register office on Wednesday; Newcombe visiting Ruby Price on Thursday; Newcombe in an argument with Frank Vicary on Sunday afternoon and shot on Sunday evening.

Ruby Price shot on Monday.

Nicholas Beale's automatic used for both killings.

These were the more obvious facts but there were others which might have to fit the pattern.

Edward saying nothing of the finding of Ruby's body for two days; Edward inventing a mysterious stranger; Edward's father, a wife-murderer.

Emily Newcombe acquiring a substantial sum of money in the early sixties.

And, unlikely as it seemed, Newcombe with a reputation for a way with the girls.

Facts, and the fancies they gave rise to, chased each other round in his head like the roundabouts at the fair. It was not a new situation; he was used to it, and usually from the mêlée an idea would emerge which could be tried and tested.

He walked across to Ashill and Joyce answered his ring. Without a word she stood aside for him to enter.

"I want to talk to Mr. Simon."

"Then you'd better go across to the maypole."

"Is he over there?"

"Why shouldn't he be? He pays for it being put up every year—or do you think he ought to hide himself because of what they're saying and doing? This morning there was chalk scribblings all over this front door, with your man out there in his van, sleeping most likely. A fat lot of good he is!" Joyce was trembling with indignation. "You and your lot have started something!"

Wycliffe made the soft answer. "There have been two murders, remember."

"You don't give us much chance to forget! Anyway, Bunny Newcombe's not much loss; that boy was never any good to anybody; his poor mother least of all."

"And Ruby Price?"

Joyce sniffed. "Well, there's plenty who'll speak well of her."

"And you?"

"I don't speak about anybody if I can help it but I can't abide busybodies who aren't satisfied with their own affairs and dabble in other people's."

"Is that what Ruby did?"

"Well, she interfered in this family. Got a hold on the mistress, poor lady." Joyce shrugged her thin shoulders. "Well, all that's over now, but Ruby had a way with her, there's no denying that. People told her their troubles; leastwise, some did; she never got anything out of me." She broke off abruptly. "But this is gossip and if it's gossip you want you've come to the wrong place. Are you stopping or going?"

"Is Mrs. Vicary at home?"

"It would be an odd thing if she wasn't; she never goes anywhere."

"Never?"

"Well, she doesn't go out much; perhaps a walk with Mr. Nicholas of an evening."

"Is there something wrong with her?"

"Why should there be? There's nothing wrong with me and I never go out—never!"

"I would like to see Mrs. Vicary."

"Then you'd better go round to the outside stairs; they don't like people using the door from the house. Of course, *he* uses it but that's different."

"Thank you."

"For what? You got nothing out of me you couldn't've got else-where."

Wycliffe went round to the side of the house where there were steps up to the first floor from the old coach-house yard. The land-ing at the top of the steps was sheltered by a canopy. He rang the bell and had to wait for some time before the door was opened by a woman in a floral housecoat. She had a mass of auburn hair and the firm but not prominent features which often go with it, but she had escaped freckles. A very attractive woman, looking surprisingly young to have a daughter of nineteen. But there were signs that all was not well; a redness and a moistness about the eyes, and spots of colour on her cheeks not entirely concealed by make-up.

Drink? Almost for certain. Wycliffe wondered what particular sorrows she found it necessary to drown.

"Mrs. Vicary? . . . Detective Chief Superintendent Wycliffe."

She took him into the drawing-room. It was furnished tradition-ally in subdued colours with fabrics of indeterminate pattern; deco-ration to match. Just about right for the executive who asks only for a neutral background. One had the impression it might have come in a package deal from somewhere not quite Harrods. Was it part of Gertrude's problem that she was expected to merge into it?

"Do sit down. You want to talk to me?"

She did not immediately sit down herself, and when she did she sat erect and remained very tense. If he was going to get her to talk he would have to reassure her first.

"I've met your daughter; she is like you."

She looked surprised. "Really? I suppose I should be flattered." But she was anxious. "What did you want to ask me about?"

"I want your help. I am going to be quite blunt. As you know, two people have been killed and it seems that the only things they have in common are their connections with this family and the fact that they were both shot with a pistol taken from your brother's room downstairs. We don't want to cause unnecessary pain or embarrass-ment. It is very easy to find ourselves prying into things about which people are naturally reticent and then misinterpreting their silence. It is much better to be frank with us. Once we are satisfied that whatever it is has no connection with our case it is forgotten."

Like the March Hare's, it was the best butter and Gertrude responded. "What is it you want to know?"

"About Ruby Price's connection with your family."

Wycliffe had expected a sudden relaxation of tension at this seeming anticlimax but there was none. Gertrude remained very wary. She took time to collect her thoughts. "Well, Ruby was a close friend of my mother's and, as a midwife, she brought us all into the world. It's as simple as that."

"If you could enlarge a little . . ."

A faint smile. "It started with my brother, Nicholas, the eldest of the family. He was born prematurely in the middle of a blizzard and Ruby was the only one who could get here. She was young at the time, not much older than Mother, and just starting as a district nurse. It was a very difficult birth and Mother believed Ruby saved her life and that of the child. Probably it was true; at any rate there grew up between them a close friendship which lasted right up until my mother's death. In fact, Ruby was with Mother when she died."

"Your mother discussed things with her—family matters?"

"Everything!" Gertrude pulled her housecoat over her knees. "Unless you kept something from Mother it was no secret from Ruby."

"Did she ever make use of your mother's confidences to cause trouble in the family?"

Gertrude frowned. "Not directly, but she had a lot of influence on Mother and we all resented that from time to time."

On a side-table, close to Wycliffe's chair, there was a silver-framed photograph of a young girl—Gertrude, as she had been at eighteen or thereabouts. People must have thought that Vicary, a clerk in her father's firm, had really hit the jackpot; this luscious girl and a stake in Beales' Household Stores. They would have wondered if he had contrived his luck by a spot of judicious seduction, but it was hard to imagine the girl Gertrude had been falling for the little man who was within easy striking distance of being ugly. But sex is a capricious ringmaster.

Wycliffe said, "Less than three weeks before she died, Ruby was visited by your brother, Nicholas. She noted the visit in her diary.

He wanted an assurance that she would not pass on certain information about him to a friend."

Wycliffe was watching her closely and he saw her relax; she even smiled and enquired, "A woman friend?"

"Probably Veronica Gould."

"Poor Nicky! So you know about that. I see now what you've come for but I'm afraid I can't help you."

Wycliffe persisted. "What I said earlier, Mrs. Vicary, was perfectly true. If we know the reason for your brother's concern and it has nothing to do with our case, there's an end to it. If we are not told we shall poke and pry until we find out."

She was suddenly bitter. "Yours must be a very rewarding occupation!"

He did not hold it against her. "Did your brother complete the full term of his army service?"

"He resigned his commission."

"Why?"

"Hadn't you better ask him that?"

He risked being blunt. "He wouldn't tell me if I did. I have the impression that your brother doesn't always act in his own best interest."

He saw her lips tremble in another smile. "You are a very shrewd man, Mr. Wycliffe, and I am going to take you at your word—that you will ignore what is not directly concerned with your case. What you say about Nicky is quite true; he is a very obstinate man. In some ways he is very innocent . . ." She searched for an expression. "I sometimes think that it is a common failing with us Beales—we are emotionally *dumb*. Anyway, enough of that! In a nutshell, Nicky made a fool of himself over a boy—young man, I suppose he was."

She reached for a box of cigarettes on a side-table. "Will you smoke?"

"No, thank you."

She lit one herself and drew on it, deeply. "Nicky had a desk job with the British garrison in Berlin and he fell for a German youth who worked in the administration. There was a liaison—isn't that the word? It's certainly the word Nicky would have used, with a disapproving twist, if it had happened to anyone else. But, of course, Nicky was trapped. It turned out the boy was a commie plant."

Gertrude tapped ash from her cigarette into a glass ashtray shaped like a swan. "I don't know if Nicky had any information which might have been useful to the Russians or to the Democratic Republic—it doesn't seem likely—but if he had, he didn't part with it to the boy. An exhaustive investigation, during which he was suspended from duty, established that much, but it was the investigation coupled with the disgrace which broke Nicky and put him, for a time, in a psychiatric hospital. What made it worse, all this happened shortly before my mother's death and Nicky feels that he shortened her life."

Wycliffe said, "Was it at all likely that Ruby Price would have passed any of this on to the Gould sisters?"

"I really don't know. Ruby certainly had no reason to be antagonistic to any of us. Of course, Nicky is a born worrier. All his life he's been convinced that somebody is about to pull the mat out from under him, so he takes precautions and, sometimes, they're a bit ponderous."

"I can see that you are very fond of him."

She smiled. "At heart he's a kindly old thing. He was my big brother when I was a kid and ever since Esther was born he's thought the world of her. Like a lot of others, he's his own worst enemy." She looked at him in a challenging way. "Well, I've done what you asked and I hope you'll keep your side of the bargain. I should hate to see Nicky having to go through any part of that again. If he's happy with his battles and his Veronica, let him have them."

Wycliffe allowed a comfortable silence to drift on for a while then he said, "I wonder if you can—or will—tell me why Nicholas is so antagonistic towards your husband?"

A faint smile. "As a fully paid up member of the clan I suppose I should say that I know of no such antagonism. In fact, of course, we all know about it. It's not surprising really. Nicholas refused to go into the firm because he knew that he would never get on with Father and also because he had no inclination for business. He joined the army instead but, as I've told you, his career there ended unpleasantly. On the other hand, my husband—an outsider—seems to be uniformly successful and enjoys my father's complete confidence. Added to that, in Nicky's eyes, I'm still his baby sister. . . . I suppose it all amounts to jealousy and sounds a bit absurd but natural all the same."

Wycliffe nodded.

"It came to a head recently when Frank offered to buy Nicholas's shares in the firm and Nicky chose to be insulted."

"Thank you for being so open with me; it helps."

Gertrude had relaxed. Her earlier fears, whatever they had been, had not materialized; now she was expecting Wycliffe to go and, no doubt, she would breathe a great sigh of relief when he did.

But Wycliffe did not go; instead he settled back in his chair and said: "A week ago yesterday, in the afternoon, Newcombe went to the register office in Newton and asked to see the entry of his birth in the register."

Gertrude became wary. "So?"

"Did your husband tell you Newcombe had been to the register office?"

"Why should he?"

He noted the evasion.

"Because after seeing the entry which referred to him he asked also for the entries covering your marriage to Mr. Vicary and the birth of your daughter."

"Is it possible for anyone to walk into a register office and see entries referring to other people?"

"Quite possibly; Newcombe did so."

She had herself well in hand and the only detectable change in her was a tensing of her muscles so that she was no longer relaxed in her chair.

"What am I supposed to make of that? I can't imagine what he hoped to gain by it."

"You can make no suggestion why the entries might have interested him?"

"I cannot. Can you?"

"Just one more question, Mrs. Vicary. Do you know of any reason why your family might have paid a substantial sum of money to the Newcombes in the early sixties?"

"I do not!"

And with that he had to be content.

He came out of the house with its oppressive tensions into the sunshine. There was a new warmth in the air; one of those spring days when it would have been good to relax, to grow nostalgic and to be easily amused, but the Beales possessed his thoughts like a toothache.

Gertrude impressed him; she was the most adult of the Beales; at the same time she was a frustrated woman, turning to drink.

"We are emotionally dumb": a graphic image calling to mind the efforts of a deaf mute to communicate—the inarticulate sounds, the despairing gestures, the sullen withdrawal. . . . It was tempting to see members of the family as being in different stages of the sequence.

On the Green the crowd had grown; they were crowning the May Queen, a dark, pretty girl who sat demurely on her throne while the chairman of the parish council, wearing his chain of office, balanced a crown of flowers on her head. A ceremony which had once linked soil fertility with human sex, but now the fields around Washford, like fields everywhere, had their fertility delivered in sacks.

Wycliffe prowled on the fringe of the crowd and reached a place where people were thinner on the ground; then he spotted Simon. It was extraordinary; Simon, standing alone, isolated in the crowd near the platform, with at least a yard of space all about him. There was something almost heroic about the tall, frail old man with the silvery hair; a patriarchal figure. Wycliffe thought the villagers would probably let him be, but when he saw a uniformed policeman standing a little apart, he warned him to keep an eye on the old man.

Washford Fair this year would receive more publicity than at any time in its history; already a TV van had moved in and was parked near the police caravans. Three or four obvious reporters, keeping aloof from the rustic celebrations, sat on a bench outside the pub, settling down to some steady drinking. One of them called to him:

"Anything fresh, Mr. Wycliffe?"

"Not a thing."

"Will you have anything for us today?"

"You tell me. Your guess is as good as mine."

Wycliffe lunched at the Mill House Hotel on the Newton road. The pub in the village was so crowded that it was all but impossible to elbow one's way to the bar. At the Mill House business was also brisk with farming families from the district having lunch before going on to the fair. Wycliffe arrived late, when most of the diners had reached their dessert and he watched, fascinated, while plump farmers, their wives and their children tucked into great wedges of Black Forest gâteau loaded with Devonshire cream.

Afterwards he walked back to the village and, for an hour, he behaved like a visitor, looking in on some of the events—a flower show in the church hall, a judo demonstration, a pony gymkhana. . . . Village life suited him; the scale was right; an audience of two or three hundred is enough for anything; get into the thousands and you have a mob. . . . Small is beautiful; he agreed with Papa Schumacher. He had read of research which showed that certain rodents become aggressive if they encounter more than a small number of their own kind in a day. He could sympathize.

Those who noticed him at all saw a middle-aged man, rather severely dressed, who looked vaguely like a priest. He smoked his pipe and watched whatever was going on with apparent interest, a contemplative interest which more restless, excitable types might have envied. They could not have guessed what was going on behind the calm, grey eyes.

The Beales: one of them is a killer. And, a little later: Is Gertrude the still centre about which it all revolves? Four days since he had first heard of Newcombe; two days since the discovery of the second killing . . . What next?

A family with a century of tradition, living in the same village, in the same house, hedged in by an oppressive respectability, isolated by religion and class, and uniquely susceptible to the frustrations, jealousies and repressions which can nurture thoughts of violence. . . . Although the two victims were not of the family he had no doubt that this was a family affair. . . .

Which of them?

Simon was an old man and frail, but no young muscles were

needed to pull the trigger of a nine-millimetre, and the crimes betrayed a calculating coldness which was probably not out of character.

Nicholas: an introvert who had already suffered a traumatic shock and now seemed destined to go through life looking over his shoulder and tilting at shadows.

Maurice: pompous and foolish; but sufficiently aware of his own shortcomings to feel threatened. Often the weak are the first to turn to violence. And Maurice had a shrewish, nagging wife.

Edward: son of a wife-murderer; inhibited, striving to express himself through paint and canvas but still well and truly knotted. Impossible to guess what went on behind that timid front.

Vicary: according to Patterson he had dropped his girl overnight to marry the boss's daughter. A man who believed in his destiny; others stand back. A blank as far as his emotional life was concerned; no cosy little woman to come home to. . . .

That left the women.

Could these crimes be the work of a woman? He saw no reason why they should not. Women have a penchant for direct, practical solutions.

Gertrude: Wycliffe saw her as a passive element, but that was only an impression. She was married to a man with whom she seemed to have nothing in common; she had retreated into herself and was finding what consolation she could in drink; but she was intelligent and shrewd. It was by no means impossible that she had decided to . . . to clear the decks? He was not satisfied with this assessment; there was more, another factor . . . sex. In talking to Gertrude he had sensed . . . he found difficulty in putting it into words, he had been conscious of a powerful yearning, a barely repressed lust. . . .

And Esther. With such parents, what might she not be? It was more than possible that her impressive air of calm detachment was a pose. Wycliffe had a daughter of his own and knew from experience that girls dramatize themselves in more subtle ways than boys. Her job in the supermarket had come as a surprise but that too could be part of the role she saw herself as playing.

Which brought him to Naomi; foolish, scheming, nagging Naomi. No killer—certainly not with a firearm.

He sighed. Conning the field is a useful exercise but it took no account of motive. Which of these people had reason to want Newcombe and Ruby Price dead?

His thoughts turned to Newcombe's cottage, where, as far as he was concerned, it had all started. It occurred to him that, because she had been murdered, Ruby Price was occupying the centre of the stage, while Emily Newcombe had scarcely been thought about. Yet, if Emily had been alive. . : . Ruby had monitored the life of the village with her scraps of paper in envelopes—living vicariously; but Emily had a son and, surely, she would have treasured mementoes of events which affected him. . . .

He worked his way back to the police van through the growing crowds. Dixon, as duty officer, was using the slack time to study for his promotion exam. Wycliffe collected and signed for the key of the cottage then walked down the lane beside Ashill, past Quarry House. No one to be seen anywhere. Only the music from the fairground disturbed the peace. The church clock chimed the three-quarters—a quarter to four.

The cottage looked as he had first seen it, the gate screeched open, but there was no commotion in the hutches and no hens pecked over the weedy yard; the livestock had been removed by the Fretwells that morning.

The key was an old-fashioned latchkey of intricate pattern suggesting a complicated lock, but Wycliffe knew from his childhood that a bit of bent wire worked just as well. He passed through the lean-to scullery into the kitchen and paused while his eyes accustomed themselves to the dim light.

The lapse of time had done nothing to mitigate the squalor or the stench, and there were more flies. He knew from the scene-of-crime inventory that Emily had kept her mementoes in the drawers of the chiffonier in the parlour. He pushed open the plank door which separated the two rooms and, for an instant, he could not believe his eyes; there, standing between him and the window, by the chiffonier, was Joyce; Joyce wearing a long coat of some dark, silky material and a felt hat which must have dated from before the war. A large, shiny handbag with a brass clasp stood on the chiffonier.

Of the two, he was the more disconcerted. She looked at him with her fierce little eyes and waited for him to speak.

He did his best to sound stern. "What are you doing here?"

"I came to have a look."

"How did you get in?"

She held up a "key" of the sort used to open sardine cans.

"Why should you want to 'look' as you call it?"

Her skin was brown, furrowed by myriads of tiny wrinkles, and she had a thin, whitish moustache; but her vitality gave her a certain compelling appeal; she could not be ignored, she could not be wholly disliked.

"I went to school with Emily; I worked with her for more than fifty years; we started at Ashill in the same week, when we was fourteen. I should think that gave me the right to have a look before *she* gets her hands on it all." Her manner was both aggressive and defensive.

"She?"

"Martha Fretwell. Martha was a Newcombe and she never had any room for Emily—thought her precious brother was too good for a common servant girl; all because, with his smarmy ways, he'd talked himself into a job as gardener at Ashill when all he really was, was a rabbit catcher. Too good for Emily! All they Newcombes was a no-account lot, and Emily's boy was no different. He was a trial to his mother and no mistake, but she thought the world of him. Now she's gone, and see what happened to him!"

Both drawers of the chiffonier were open; one contained the sort of things to be found in such drawers in thousands of homes everywhere; letters preserved in their envelopes, postcards, programmes of local events, a pad of lined writing paper and a couple of ball-point pens; a few envelopes. The other drawer held a photograph album, a collection of cigarette cards in a cardboard box, a couple of board games and a pack of playing cards.

"What were you looking for?"

"I wasn't looking *for* anything, I was looking at Emily's photos. Emily was a great one for photos. I remember the first thing she bought when she'd saved a bit of money was a camera—one of those box ones. I remember it was called a 2A Brownie and she said it took bigger pictures."

Wycliffe hardly knew whether to laugh or be angry. He said, "You know you've no right here."

She bristled. "I've as much right here as Martha Fretwell—more! I done what I could for Emily when she was alive—I used to come down here when she was ill and try to keep the place something like. Not Martha! She wouldn't soil her hands for anybody else's benefit. All this"—she pointed to the contents of the drawers—"Martha won't give it house room but she won't let them have it as would."

Joyce had dressed for the occasion and she smelt of lavender. She had on a mauve blouse under her coat, caught at the neck with a cameo brooch; she even wore shoes though these made a concession to her bunions by having elastic insertions in the toe caps.

Wycliffe lifted out the photograph album and opened it on top of the chiffonier. Like most of its kind it lacked any labels to the photographs. He turned the pages, stopping now and then for Joyce's comments on the pictures.

"That's the servants at Ashill—Emily got Mr. Simon to take that. Of course, he was only a youngster then like we was and his father was still alive. That's Emily and that's me . . ."

A little *gamine*, pert and full of life.

"That's the cook and that's Mrs. Endacott, the housekeeper; we was four of us living in then with two daily maids. . . . That's Mr. Simon and the mistress when they came back from their honeymoon. Don't you think they made a lovely couple? Newcombe with his father . . ."

There were several photographs of the Beales, both as children and growing up, individually and in groups. Sometimes young Newcombe was photographed with the Beale brothers in the woods. Even as teenagers Maurice was the stout one with an expression which seemed to suggest a permanent if vague protest; Nicholas was long and lean and his features expressed nothing at all.

"The Beale brothers seemed to get on well enough with young Newcombe."

Joyce sniffed. "Oh, they did. Newcombe and his father saw to that; they knew which side their bread was buttered. They used to take the boys out shooting; they showed them how to set traps and snares, where to find different nests, and sometimes they went on badger hunts. You can't lose if you get boys with that sort of thing."

One or two of the snapshots showed Gertrude with her teenaged brothers; a little mop-haired girl in a bib-and-brace overall, clearly determined to be left out of nothing. Wycliffe continued to turn the pages but there were no more pictures of the Beale brothers. Presumably Nicholas had gone into the army and Maurice was starting work with the firm.

On one of the pages near the end of the album there was a blank where a picture had been removed, leaving the corners.

"What happened to that one?"

Joyce shrugged. "How should I know?"

It had been an idle question but the tone of Joyce's response roused his suspicion.

"I think you do know."

"I can't stop you thinking."

He pointed to her handbag. "Let me see."

She was about to refuse, but thought better of it. "All right! I took it because I got a better right to it than Martha Fretwell. She'll burn the lot."

He held out his hand.

Reluctantly she opened her handbag and took out a print which she laid on the album. "It's Miss Gertrude at eighteen or thereabouts. She never kept many of her photos and I wanted it to remind me of what she was like before . . . before she was married."

"She's with Newcombe!"

"Well, I can't help that, can I? I expect that's why Emily took it. I thought I could have him cut off and the rest enlarged. A proper photographer could do that, couldn't he?"

Joyce was uncharacteristically garrulous.

Wycliffe said, "Yes, I think so," but he was preoccupied with the snapshot itself. Gertrude, in a jumper and skirt, stood sideways to the camera, she was smiling at Newcombe, lips parted; Newcombe had a rather strained expression on his face while a little bird, its wings blurred by motion too rapid for the film speed, seemed to be feeding from his lips.

Joyce said, "He could do that sort of thing; he had a way with all sorts of animals. He could bring down most any bird from the trees by imitating its call but 'twasn't because he was fond of them; it was just a knack."

Wycliffe was not paying her any attention; the snapshot seemed to fascinate him. If Gertrude had been eighteen at the time, Newcombe would have been twenty-three. He didn't look it. He had filled out since the earlier snaps but he was still not fat, and Wycliffe was reminded of a young bull; earthy and vigorous.

Suddenly a key piece seemed to fall into place; it was all so obvious; the answer had been under his nose from the start. Joyce was aware of the change in him and she stood, waiting; there was no longer any point in her barrage of chatter.

Wycliffe looked at the little old woman with something like awe. "You know the whole story; you've known it all along; that's why you're here. . . ."

She made an irritable movement. "I've no idea what you're talking about but I can't spend all day hanging about; they have their meal early on fair nights and it's time I was back there."

He didn't argue. "One question and you can go." He pointed to the pale rectangle on the wall where the damaged picture had hung and he showed her the frame. "What was in that?"

She hesitated, but not for long. "It was the same photo, but bigger. Emily had it enlarged." She moved to the door but as she reached it she turned back; she said in a manner that was more cautionary than aggressive: "You think you've found out something, but you could still get it wrong."

With that, she went, through the kitchen and the scullery, her steps a little unsure because of the shoes. Wycliffe put the snapshot in his wallet. He thought that he now knew all that the cottage had to tell him; he was no longer casting about in the dark; he had a motive of sorts and the framework of a case. What remained to be done, he told himself, was routine police work.

He let himself out by the back door, closing it by the absurd drop-latch. As he came out into the yard the church clock chimed the half-hour—half past four; he could hear it plainly above the subdued cacophony from the fairground.

He stood in the yard, looking at the accumulated litter of years, at the moss-grown walls and the nettles. Probably Newcombe would have spent the rest of his life in these surroundings with the place slowly crumbling and decaying before his eyes—and been more or less content. But something had stirred him to uncharacteristic activity and the climax seemed to have been reached on Sunday afternoon, the day of his death, when Rose Gould had passed by with her little dog and overheard Vicary laying down the law: "You've done very well out of this, Newcombe!" And a little later, "If you adopt that attitude, Newcombe, you are making the biggest mistake of your life!" And that evening Newcombe had been shot.

On the previous Wednesday he had been at the register office in Newton, and on the Thursday, he was calling on the former midwife. On the day following Newcombe's death the midwife had been killed in the same manner. It had been his job to find the links between these events and to establish a clear, unambiguous motive for the violence. For the first time he seemed to be making progress.

He decided to walk back through the estate, so he climbed the wall once more and followed the path made by the dead man. He came to the clearing and to Quarry House, which looked deserted in the sunshine though assailed by raucous sounds from the fairground and the incessant roar of the waterfall. Wycliffe climbed the steps to the top, to the little pavilion which bridged the stream at the head of the fall. From the veranda he could see down into the Goulds' garden but there was no one about. He heard a slight sound behind him and turned sharply; it was Esther. She had come from the house and had been startled to find him there.

"Did you want something?" Her manner was edgy.

"No, I'm on my way back from the cottage. I gather you are no longer troubled by the livestock."

She smiled. "The Fretwells didn't waste time in shifting the rabbits and hens."

Wycliffe glanced through the window at the little room with its summer-house atmosphere. "Do you spend much time down here?"

"No. When we were younger—Edward and I, we used to come

down here sometimes; there was a row-boat on the pool and once or twice we went swimming, but it was always very cold."

He was seeing the girl with new eyes and, not for the first time in his career, he marvelled at the quirky nature of inheritance. But no other explanation was possible.

When he got back to the Green it was crowded with people watching a fancy-dress competition in which the contestants paraded along a raised gangway before a panel of judges. Wycliffe saw the inevitable Walt Disney characters with a little fat boy as Dumbo and two Snow Whites. He had difficulty in working his way through the crowd to the roped-off area where the caravans and police vehicles were parked and when he reached the van he was more relieved than he would have been prepared to admit to find Kersey there.

Kersey listened and his first reaction was incredulity. "You mean that girl is his?"

"Yes."

Kersey needed time to allow the idea to sink in. He reached into his pocket and came out with a packet of cigarettes. He took one out, stroked it between finger and thumb and lit it as though performing a ritual act. "As the French say on their diarrhoea pills, 'one in moments of crisis.' I must admit the possibility never occurred to me." He added, after a longish pause, "Do you think she knows?"

"I've no idea."

Kersey was thinking aloud. "If Newcombe had come out into the open it would only have been his word against the others. . . . I suppose he was looking for corroboration in a ham-fisted sort of way, and we've now got the same problem. . . . There's no way of proving it unless someone talks."

Wycliffe said, "This isn't a paternity case, it's murder; but now we have a possible motive, or a complex of motives centred on the girl's parentage."

Kersey was enjoying the luxury of allowing the smoke to trickle between his lips, watching it rise in thin spirals. He said, "That motive points straight to Vicary."

Wycliffe looked dubious. "It's not that simple. Even allowing that Newcombe was able to persuade Vicary to take him seriously—

seriously enough for Vicary to feel threatened and to go for murder
—that doesn't explain why Ruby Price was killed."

"Ruby was the only one outside the family who knew the truth.
With Newcombe murdered and the weapon a pistol from Ashill, it
wouldn't have taken her long to put two and two together. . . .
Vicary must have seen that risk; he may even have talked to her,
sounding her out."

"He would have had to get a move on. Newcombe was shot on
Sunday night, Ruby on Monday afternoon."

Kersey shrugged. "Well, he couldn't allow the grass to grow under
his feet if he had any doubts, could he?"

"You make him out as a cold-blooded killer."

"He's an accountant—green ink instead of blood."

Wycliffe got out his pipe and started to fill it. "I'll go this far with
you: Vicary is our best bet at the moment."

"So how do we go?"

"With caution; we haven't a shred of proof. When he comes
home I'll talk to him."

Through the little window they could see, over the heads of the
crowd, other fancy-dress characters parading along the gangway; a
Pink Panther and an overfed Snoopy.

Wycliffe got to his feet. "According to Joyce the family dine early
on fair night; Vicary may be home already." He crossed the little
room to the door, then turned back, "I want the house put under
observation; the main gates and the entrance in South Street which
they use when they're driving."

"I'll see to it, sir."

He entered Ashill by the main gates, walked round the house and up
the steps to the first-floor flat. He had to wait some time before the
door was opened by Gertrude. Gertrude looking flushed, her eyes
surrounded by puffiness. She had obviously been sleeping, probably
after several drinks, but she did her best to appear normal. "Was it
me you wanted?"

"Your husband."

"Frank?" She seemed surprised. "He's not at home; it's Friday."

"Friday?"

A faint smile. "Frank doesn't come home on Friday evenings; he goes straight off from the office."

"Where?"

He must have conveyed a sense of urgency. "Is there something wrong; has something happened?"

"I simply want to talk to your husband. Where is he likely to be?"

"I've no idea." She looked blank.

"Your husband goes somewhere every Friday evening, straight from the office, but you've no idea where?"

"That's what I said." Very curt. She was recovering her poise and beginning to resent his manner.

"What time do you expect him back?"

"He's usually back around midnight."

"He isn't interested in the fair?"

"It would take more than the fair to change Frank's routine."

"Thank you."

He was irritated, almost angry; these people must *know*. Then, when the door had closed behind him he wondered, What did they know? Who knew, and what? Who was suspected, and by whom? It was one thing to build a wall; quite another to have to live behind it. He tried to imagine them sitting down to a meal together.

As a boy he had often walked past the walls of country houses and looked down tree-lined drives to catch a glimpse of imposing gables. He had thought then that the people on the other side must live story-book lives; lives of dignified leisure, with mutual tolerance filled with innocent pleasures.

On an impulse, perhaps in reaction to a surfeit of Beales, he telephoned his wife: "You don't feel like coming over to the fair? I have to be here and I shall probably have to stay half the night . . . yes, I had a very good lunch . . . no, you can't bring cars into the village now the fair is on—only residents'; you park somewhere along the Newton road and walk up South Street to the Green. Our caravan is on the Green opposite the church. . . . About seven? I'll be there, waiting for you. . . . Take care!"

By tradition they dined early at Ashill on fair day and, despite the air of gloomy foreboding which pervaded the house, perhaps because of it, seven of the usual eight places were occupied; only Vicary was absent. The music from the fairground and the cumulative mutterings and shufflings of a great crowd of people reached them as a confused murmur, punctuated by an occasional shout, a raucous laugh, or the cry of a child. There was scarcely any conversation and as soon as the meal of cold meat and salad was over the party broke up.

Gertrude, looking like a woman in a somnambulent trance, went back to the flat. Naomi, with elaborate concern, said, "Of course, you won't be going out, Father, will you?"

The old man turned to look at her and let his gaze linger for a while before saying, "Why not?"

"I think you would be most unwise, the way things are! With a good deal of drink about the villagers might turn really nasty. I mean, look what . . ." Her words faded under his cold stare.

Esther said, "Are you coming, Edward?"

Naomi pounced. "Edward! You're not going out, surely?"

Edward looked as though every drop of blood had been drained from his body; he mumbled something incoherent and followed Esther from the room.

Naomi sighed. "Well, *I'm* not going out. I wouldn't feel safe! In fact, I think the police ought to give us more effective protection here."

Maurice said, "I shall have to spend an hour or so on our estimates for the next half-year but after that . . ." He turned to his brother. "What about you, Nicky?"

Nicholas had gone over to the window, where he stood, looking out. "I shall be going out later."

"Then let's go together. What about it?" Maurice laughed self-consciously. "Recapture the days of our youth. Remember fair night in the old days, Nicky?"

Nicholas said, "Those days are gone."

By nine-thirty only the three women were left in the house.

In the big drawing-room downstairs, Naomi sat by an electric fire placed in the large, open grate. She was playing patience on a low table. The heavy red-velvet curtains were drawn and two chandeliers blazed with light, but with so little reflection from the walls and furnishings, the room still had a gloomy aspect. Naomi's plump little hands manipulated the cards and her short, tapering fingers hovered like a bird of prey, ready to pounce.

In her own little sitting-room Joyce was watching television; she had kicked off her slippers and her stockinged feet rested on a padded stool.

Gertrude, in the drawing-room of the flat, sat in darkness except for the flicker of the television screen. She had not bothered to draw the curtains and a faintly luminous sky with a silhouette of trees was visible through the window panes. It was impossible to say whether or not she slept; she lay back in her chair, her lips slightly parted, motionless; her lids drooped but were probably not quite closed.

Washford Horse and Hiring Fair was entering its last hours and not a horse had been traded nor a man hired but it had been an enjoyable day and it was not over yet.

As darkness fell a swathe of brilliance cut through the whole village from the top of North Street to the Green; the stalls which lined the street were selling everything from handbags and sexy nighties to farm boots and overalls. The stall holders came from far afield; some were cockneys who made it their business to follow the country fairs. Two streams of people flowed sluggishly up and down the street, congealing round certain stalls then moving on again. The fun-fair in Church Field was a source of even more brilliant light and more raucous sound, glaring and blaring into the night, while the big wheel turned majestically, carrying its passengers up, briefly, into the darkness.

The Wycliffes worked their way conscientiously along the stalls.

"Floral pattern, bone-china tea-service—twenty pieces: worth thirty pounds of anybody's money. . . . But I'm not asking thirty . . . not twenty . . . not fifteen . . ."

"Knickers, step-ins, scanties, panties, briefs—whatever you call 'em it don't make no difference to me; they all cover the same ground if you get my meaning, an' I bin selling 'em at Washford Fair for fifteen year an' my ol' man before that. The chances are your granny bought 'er passion bafflers from my ol' man an' my God! she needed 'em wiv' 'im about . . ."

"Sheets, ladies! Cotton sheets! None of yer nylon rubbish; none of yer Hong Kong rejects—I'm off'ring you real Egyptian cotton sheets—feel 'em lady! Soft as a baby's bottom . . ."

Helen said, "We could do with some sheets."

"But not here; you'll get done."

"I don't see why; he's handing them around for people to feel."

"All right; if you like."

"You go on, I'll pick you up later."

"In this crowd?"

"We can fix a place." Helen was not sorry to have a chance to do the stalls at her own pace.

"All right. Let's say by the old organ in the fairground. But watch out for bag-snatchers."

Wycliffe drifted with the crowd, moving towards the Green: a similar stream moved in the opposite direction; there were bottle-necks but people edged their way through with good humour. He had to admit that he was enjoying himself. He did not want to do or see anything in particular, it was enough to be part of this—he searched for a word—of this procession, for that is what it seemed to be: all these people, each following their own bent but part of a pattern of movement as regular and symmetrical as if it had been choreographed. Down the street, around the Green, into the fair-ground, out of the fairground, around the Green, up the street . . .

The police caravans were lit up and, with a number of other police vehicles, had been taped off from the crowd. Wycliffe was borne along past it, past the churchyard with its gloomy yews, and into the fairground. He carried a personal radio so that he could be called if necessary and he had left instructions that he was to be told if Vicary returned.

An old-fashioned fairground organ was playing a Sousa march and canned "pop" music came from amplifiers in confusing discord, punctuated by banshee wails which accompanied some of the riders. A stall selling candy floss, another nougat. The nougat stall brought back memories; his mother had disapproved of sweets in general but excepted barley sugar and nougat, both of which he disliked, so that fairs were forever associated in his mind with the chewy, sticky, rather sickly sweetness of nougat.

A shooting gallery, darts and hoopla, all with elusive prizes which looked much the same as they had done forty years ago; a wrestling booth; a Tunnel of Terror. . . . His first visit to a fairground in twenty years and he felt like a time traveller. The chair-o-planes looked more dangerous and masqueraded under another name; there was a whirling Noah's Ark; dodgems where the lads of the village were giving their aggro a fairly harmless airing; and a devilish contraption which whipped screaming couples round at dizzy speeds in wavering orbits.

Wycliffe stopped to watch and spotted Maurice; Maurice in a tight-fitting, lightweight overcoat which made him look more paunchy than he was. He was gazing at the whirling couples with a lost look.

"Good evening, Mr. Beale."

Maurice started and turned toward him. "Oh, it's you, Superintendent! I don't suppose you've seen my father? I'm just a bit concerned; he's so self-willed and he's not as young as he was. . . . I met Esther earlier and she said she'd seen him pottering around the stalls in North Street, but it's hopeless looking for anyone in the crush up there."

"No, I haven't seen your father, Mr. Beale, but are you seriously worried?"

Maurice looked vague. "Not seriously—no. In fact, I think he is quite capable of looking after himself but my wife . . ."

Maurice was like a fat schoolboy pretending to be grown up and vaguely aware that he was not making a good job of it.

Wycliffe said, "I wanted to talk to Mr. Vicary but I understand he isn't home this evening."

Maurice frowned. "My brother-in-law is never at home on Friday evenings."

"So your sister told me. Do you know where he goes?"

Maurice thought this went beyond the bounds of common politeness and his tone was a rebuke. "I have no idea."

"Business or pleasure, do you think?"

"Really, Superintendent!"

"I'm afraid you will have to get used to the idea that this is a murder enquiry, Mr. Beale. I have to ask questions."

Maurice was about to protest but changed his mind. "I suppose you must do your job as you think best."

"So, in your view, business or pleasure?"

"All I can say is that there is no business connected with the firm that would take him away on Friday evenings."

"Thank you."

Maurice was unhappy. "That doesn't mean—"

"It doesn't mean what, Mr. Beale?"

"That there is anything improper going on. After all, my brother-in-law works very hard, as I do, and he is entitled to some relaxation."

"Of course!"

Maurice went off with a very formal "Good night, Superintendent," and Wycliffe made his way through the crowds to the old organ. Once it had been the centre of whirling gondolas or dragons or galloping horses, now it stood alone on its trailer, but it still churned out the same music—marches and dance tunes of the twenties, selections from the early musicals: *Chu-Chin-Chow, The Desert Song* and *The Maid of the Mountains* . . .

A gorgeous automaton dressed like a cavalier, in green embroidered with gold, was perched in front of the gilded pipes, beating time with his baton and turning his head jerkily from side to side. He was flanked by massed trumpets, banks of shining brass, which blared forth whenever the score allowed. Above, a pyramid of bells jerked up and down to provide a tinkling counterpoint, and below, a battery of drums thumped out the rhythm.

Wycliffe glanced at his watch. Half-past ten. Helen arrived a few minutes later with a bulging polyethylene bag.

"I bought two pairs; they really are good value."

"What shall we do now?"

Arm in arm they toured the fairground and stopped at a stall selling Washford fairings—little cakes filled with whortleberry jam and served hot so that the jam spurted out, burning unwary lips. They ate four between them and tidied up each other's faces afterwards.

Helen said, "Like when we started. Do you remember Dickie Perks's fish and chips?"

As they left the fairground Wycliffe saw Simon going in through the gates of Ashill. Late return of the prodigal: it was twenty minutes to midnight. Not far off a couple of uniformed men were keeping an eye on the crowd. Wycliffe's man, logging the comings and goings through the main gates of Ashill, did so from the comparative comfort of a cubicle in the police van; his mate, responsible for the South Street entrance, was parked down there in an unmarked Mini.

Wycliffe said to Helen, "I'll call in at the van to see how things are."

D.C. Potter, duty officer, was reading the *Daily Mirror* and slurping instant coffee from a handleless mug. The radio simmered quietly, coming to life in sporadic exchanges.

"Anything to report?"

Potter tried to look efficient, which was too difficult in the circumstances, and he gave up. "Yes, sir. Radio message from D.C. Moss on obo at the South Street entrance: Vicary drove into the yard a few minutes ago." Potter checked with his report sheet. "Moss logged his return at twenty-three forty-five hours, sir."

Wycliffe picked up the clipboard and glanced through the entries. The picture seemed clear enough: Maurice and Simon had left Ashill by the main gate within twenty minutes of each other, between eight and half-past. They had returned the same way, Maurice at ten forty-five, Simon at eleven-forty.

Edward and Esther had left together also by the main gate at seven-fifteen; Edward had arrived back by nine-fifteen, Esther by nine forty-five. Now, with Vicary accounted for, the books were balanced; all safely tucked up. According to the record, Naomi, Nicholas, Gertrude and Joyce had not ventured out.

Wycliffe hesitated; he had intended to question Vicary immediately on his return but it was almost midnight; unlike some of his colleagues he was reluctant to disrupt a household at night. It could wait until morning.

He rejoined Helen. "I'm coming with you." He looked round at the crowds moving to and from the fun-fair across the Green, hemming in the police vehicles. "It won't be possible to get my car out of this lot for another hour so we'd better use yours. There's only one snag, I shall have to use yours in the morning and get somebody to drive it back . . ."

"Be my guest."

They walked down South Street, past the wide entrance to Ashill, and a disconsolate copper in his Mini, facing a lonely night. On the Newton road where Helen had left her car there was a line of parked vehicles as far as the eye could see in both directions.

The little engine of Helen's Metro spluttered into life; she made skilful use of the few inches her neighbours had left her and got clean away. By half past twelve they were home.

"Cocoa?" Helen had great faith in the soporific powers of cocoa.

"I think I'll have a nightcap instead."

He soon fell asleep but then he dreamed, a disturbing dream in which Simon was accusing him of professional misconduct for failing to fill out certain forms. Very put out, he went to call on Simon and was standing on the doorstep at Ashill, ringing the bell. Although he could hear it ringing insistently inside, no one came to answer the door.

He was awakened by Helen reaching over him to switch off the alarm clock.

"It can't be that time already!"

"Six-thirty—you set the alarm. Did you have a good sleep?"

"I don't know; I didn't have time to notice."

Downstairs, he telephoned the incident van at Washford. Potter had gone off duty and been replaced by Dixon.

"Anything to report?"

"Not a thing, sir."

At a quarter past seven he dialled the Vicarys' number. Vicary would be about. He listened while the brr-brr repeated itself a dozen or so times then a weary childish voice said, simply, "Yes?"

Esther, prised from sleep.

"This is Superintendent Wycliffe."

A moment to adjust. "Has something happened?"

"Not as far as I know; I want to speak to your father."

"I'll get him . . ."

Lilliputian sounds, then her voice, more anxious, "His bed hasn't been slept in; he can't have come home last night!"

Wycliffe hesitated. "You expected him back?"

"I'll ask Mother."

Another interval.

"She says she certainly expected him back!"

"I'll be right over."

Something adrift; either the man on obo had been seeing things or . . .

No time for more than a cup of coffee. Helen came out to see him off and grumbled when he muffed the gears on her Metro. It was foggy, low clouds blanketed every hill; on the motorway out of the city there was little traffic, only heavy lorries which seemed to be playing tag in the lanes. He arrived in Washford as the church clock chimed the hour—eight o'clock. The grey light was bringing a reluctant village back to life on the morning after; paper and plastic litter everywhere, under the drooping flags. The kitchen-midden mentality.

Dixon came out to his car. "Mr. Maurice has been over, sir, and says would you kindly come to the front door."

A family reception.

Chapter Seven

As in his dream Wycliffe found himself standing on the front steps of Ashill, ringing the doorbell; but unlike his dream, the bell was answered almost at once. Maurice came to the door, dressed much as Wycliffe had seen him in the office, not a hair out of place, but a very agitated Maurice.

"I'm glad you've come, Superintendent; it's so difficult to know . . ." His voice trailed off.

Wycliffe was taken into the gloomy drawing-room, which in the morning light seemed more sombre than ever. Edward, wearing jeans and a paint-stained shirt, was standing by the fireplace, looking lost. Simon was there in a plum-coloured silk dressing-gown. His thin neck and wrists and his mop of silvery hair gave an impression of an elegant scarecrow. He looked haggard and pale, his eyes seemed to have lost their restless vitality and the gaze he turned on Wycliffe was tired and lifeless.

Simon said, "Good of you to come, Superintendent. . . . Perhaps this is a storm in a teacup—God knows, I hope so." He raised his arms and let them fall to his sides in a gesture of helplessness.

Wycliffe felt sorry for the old man and shocked by the change in him, but surely this was overreaction to the event unless . . .

Simon himself seemed to feel the need to justify his concern. "I suppose at any time we should be worried, but in view of what has been happening one fears the worst."

"Do you know where Mr. Vicary usually spends his Friday evenings?"

"I have no idea. I gather you put that question to Maurice last night; did you have any particular reason for asking it then?"

Wycliffe avoided an answer and turned to Maurice, "When did you last see Mr. Vicary?"

Maurice cleared his throat. "Yesterday afternoon; he came into my office at about five and said that he was leaving. That was quite usual, he always leaves early on Friday."

"Did he seem worried, or in any way different to usual?"

"No, he was just as he always is."

Wycliffe returned to the old man. "Where is your other son, Mr. Beale?"

"Nicholas? Oh, he's gone off for one of his morning walks. He often gets up early and goes out."

"Does he know that his brother-in-law has not come home?"

Simon was dismissive. "I shouldn't think so for a moment!"

Maurice intervened. "He does know. I told him."

Wycliffe remembered that the police log had not recorded Nicholas leaving the estate that morning.

"Has your son-in-law ever before stayed out all night without letting anyone know?"

"Never! It is quite unlike him."

"Where is Mrs. Vicary now?"

"In their flat; my daughter-in-law is with her and, of course, Esther."

"I would like to talk to her."

Simon insisted on taking him up to the flat. He led the way upstairs, pausing now and then to recover his breath.

In the Vicarys' drawing-room Wycliffe was surprised to find the lights still on and the curtains drawn, though outside it was broad day.

Gertrude was in her dressing-gown but Naomi was fully dressed and she had taken some opportunity to put on her usual make-up. Esther, in black pants and a white shirt, sat on the hearthrug looking balletic, but she was pale with dark circles under her eyes.

Wycliffe said, "I think it would be best for me to talk to Mrs. Vicary and Esther alone."

Simon was looking round the room as though slightly bemused, probably because he was rarely in this part of the house; people came to Simon, he did not go to them.

Naomi said, "Come, Father, I think we are in the way," and Simon, with unaccustomed docility, allowed himself to be guided away. At the door Naomi paused. "I'll be back later, Gertie; after I've got things organized downstairs. Try not to worry; I'm sure it will all come out right."

Gertrude showed neither interest nor gratitude and when they were gone she turned to Wycliffe. "I suspect you dislike family conferences as much as I do."

"In my experience they take a long time to get anywhere." He went on, "You told me yesterday you had no idea where your husband went on Friday evenings; is that the truth?"

"Yes, it is." She was on edge, making an effort to control a tendency to jerkiness in her movements.

"And you, Esther—do you know?"

"Me?" She looked surprised. "I haven't the least idea where he goes." She got up from the rug, crossed to the window and swept back the curtains, letting in the harsh morning light.

Gertrude said, "Frank is system personified, his whole life runs to a schedule; the only difference between last night and any other Friday was that he didn't come home." She spoke of her husband with an exaggerated tolerance that was little short of contempt.

"You and your husband do not share a room?"

"No." She seemed to find the question natural in the circumstances.

"Then you don't know what time he comes home as a general rule?"

"Yes, I do. Often though not always, I am still awake and we exchange a few words. Invariably it is around midnight."

"So you didn't realize he hadn't returned until I telephoned and spoke to Esther?"

"No, of course not."

"And, after I telephoned, you raised the alarm downstairs." He said this in a slightly provocative way, which was not lost on her.

She answered, poker-faced, "In many ways, we are a closely knit family, Mr. Wycliffe, and my father likes to be treated as head of the house."

"Are you seriously concerned about your husband?"

She took her time, then she said, "Something must have happened to prevent him following his usual routine." The words were carefully chosen.

Wycliffe went to the window and stood, looking down into the yard and at the roofs of buildings which had been the coach-house and stables.

"Have you checked to see if his car is back?"

"How can it be?"

"It would be as well to make sure. If Esther will come down with me . . ."

Without a word Esther went to the door and held it open for him. They went through the hall and down the stairs. Several cars were housed in an open-fronted shed.

Esther said, "His car *is* there! I don't understand." She pointed to a dark-blue Rover saloon, neatly parked in its bay.

"Whose are the other cars?"

"The Volvo is Grandfather's; the BMW belongs to Uncle Maurice; the Metro is Aunt Naomi's; one of the Minis is mine and the other is Edward's. Mother and Uncle Nicholas don't have cars; they never go anywhere."

He was no nearer understanding this girl; such an odd blend of reserve and childish candour.

"Do you really have no idea where your father spends Friday evenings?"

She was silent for so long that he thought she had decided not to answer, then she said, "You think he's got a woman somewhere and you may be right, but that's not what Mother thinks—not that she would care."

"Do you?"

Her answer was sharp. "It's nothing whatever to do with me!"

He said: "Tell your mother I shall be back shortly; then I would like to talk to her alone."

She glanced at her watch. "I should be at work."

"Not today; telephone them."

She didn't argue.

He walked round the house and out through the gates to the van. St. Dorothea had withdrawn her protection, it was not actually raining but the air was saturated. Men from the council were sweeping up the litter and feeding it into a truck. The fair was over; Washford was returning to normal for another year—except for the murders.

Kersey arrived. "I've just heard about Vicary—has he done a bunk?"

"I've no idea. Moss logged him in by the South Street entrance at a quarter to twelve, but Moss is off duty. I want you to get hold of him and find out whether he identified the car, the man, or both. The car is in the yard where he usually keeps it."

Kersey rubbed his chin which, even first thing in the morning, looked like "Before" in a razor commercial. "So he's still somewhere on the estate or he's gone off on foot."

"Or he's been given a lift or been spirited away by little green men." Wycliffe was irritable. "He may be dead for all we know and, by the same token, somebody else could have driven the car back. I doubt if Moss would have noticed. Anyway, get hold of Smith and let him give the car a good going-over. As a precaution I think we should organize some sort of search of the estate—say four men, and let them work down through the woods from the back of Quarry House."

He was delayed in returning to Ashill by the telephone. Crime in the two counties had not come to a halt while he devoted himself to the Washford affair. He spoke to his deputy—John Scales, now chief inspector—and between them they settled a few queries. Afterwards he had Administrator Bellings on the line about some piddling organization problem which could have waited until the Pentecostalists take over the KGB. He thanked God that in three months Bellings would be moving to pastures new.

"I'm going back to Ashill."

When Gertrude answered his ring she had changed her dressing gown for a housecoat and she had done her hair, but she was not wearing make-up and she looked haggard.

"No news?"

"I'm afraid not. I expect Esther told you that his car is in the yard."

"She did. I can't begin to understand . . ."

In the hall he said, "I would like to check to see whether any of his clothes are missing—if he has packed a bag. Will you be able to tell?"

She seemed mildly offended. "We are married and we do still live in the same house! If you will come with me . . ."

She led the way across the hall. "This is his bedroom."

A small, plainly furnished room with a single bed and built-in cupboards. Gertrude slid back the cupboard doors on an adequate but by no means lavish stock of clothes, everything laid out with care. Suits, shirts, socks and ties were all in shades of grey; the man seemed to be obsessed with ideas of cryptic colouration.

Gertrude checked the hangers. "As far as I can see he's taken nothing with him—only the suit and the raincoat he wore to work yesterday." She slid open another cupboard which held a couple of travelling-cases and some items of smaller luggage. "There's nothing missing from there either."

Wycliffe glanced over a shelf of books at the head of the bed: novels by C. P. Snow and John Le Carré mixed in with the memoirs of politicians and civil servants. Like the rest of the room it was of almost virginal innocence.

"Does your husband have another room—office or study?"

"He uses the room next to this as an office—do you want to see it?" Her manner was detached, perhaps challenging.

The office was little more than a box-room and spartan in its furnishing: a green-metal desk with a filing cabinet and shelves to match. Wycliffe pottered about the room, glancing at the books on the shelves, opening drawers and fingering through files. Two drawers of the three-drawer cabinet were taken up with papers concerning the firm, the third was personal and domestic.

Gertrude stood by the door, watching him. "You'll find in that drawer a detailed record of my household expenditure over twenty years."

He turned his attention to the desk and skimmed through the drawers. Nothing to suggest that Vicary was other than industrious, methodical and boring.

"Do you and your husband have a joint banking account on which either of you can draw?"

She smiled. "That's the theory."

"You attend board meetings of the firm?"

"Frank holds my proxy."

Back in the hall she said, "When you came I was just about to make some coffee—would you like some?"

"Please."

"Then you'd better come into the kitchen."

Not a dream kitchen straight from the third floor of Beales' Stores but a fairly homely place; not too clean, but not filthy; not tidy, but not littered.

She busied herself with the percolator and he talked to her back.

"You couldn't make an informed guess about where your husband spends his Friday evenings?"

"I could not."

"Has he ever stayed away like this before?"

"Never."

"Do you think it's a woman?"

"I should be very surprised."

"You don't seem unduly worried."

"I hope that nothing has happened to him."

He was sitting on a stool at a plastic-topped table and he felt oddly at home. In a certain way Gertrude was his kind of woman; in other circumstances she might have been another Helen, but she had allowed herself to be packaged young; property of family and firm; a negotiable asset. In her circumstances would Helen have turned to drink and spent her time dozing in front of the television? To be honest he found it difficult to imagine Helen having got herself into Gertrude's position.

She turned and their eyes met; he wondered if she had somehow caught the drift of his thoughts. She was intelligent enough.

She put the percolator on the table, two pottery mugs, milk and sugar. "Pour your own, how you like it." She sat down opposite him.

Her housecoat opened as she sat down, showing her breasts, but she ignored it. Provocative or indifferent? From his wallet he took out the snapshot of her with Newcombe and passed it over. She took it, glanced at it and frowned. "What am I supposed to say to that?"

Her relaxed manner was a façade; little lines of strain showed on her forehead and round her mouth, and her hands were never still.

"I caught Joyce trying to smuggle it out of Newcombe's cottage yesterday. I gather there used to be a framed enlargement on the wall in the parlour but that has been taken away or destroyed."

She said, "When my brothers and I were children we spent a lot of time down there. Emily and her husband both worked for us and Morley was the same age as Maurice. He had a wonderful way with animals and it was natural—"

She was overanxious. Wycliffe interrupted, "You were no child when that was taken. Eighteen? About that, and your brothers must have been working—Nicholas in the army; Maurice in the firm."

She was eyeing him closely and Wycliffe noticed that she had not touched her coffee.

"So what? We didn't just sever relations. . . . I still went down to the cottage quite often. Why not? You seem to be trying to make something out of nothing."

He looked at her, holding her gaze until she looked away, embarrassed, then he said, "I know about Esther."

"About Esther?" But her innocence was unconvincing.

"It has taken me too long to see what was fairly obvious. I've no proof now. As Newcombe found, proof is hard to come by, but proof is one thing, certainty another. No doubt we shall get further when we start asking the right questions. . . . But what puzzles me is why two people had to die. Even if your secret had leaked out at the time it would have been hardly more than a nine-day wonder for the gossips; now, twenty years later, if Newcombe had talked, who would have believed him? Some would have pretended to, but would it have mattered? He realized this himself, otherwise there would have been no point in his clumsy efforts to get corroboration —his visit to the register office and his approach to Ruby Price."

They faced each other across the table, Gertrude sat motionless, then Wycliffe said, "Emily kept her bargain for the better part of twenty years but with his mother dead, Newcombe was free to go his own way. . . . Did he try to blackmail you or your husband?"

She shook her head but said nothing.

"In my village the father was expected to marry the girl or help to support the child, but in this case both alternatives were unthinkable; the risk here was that the father might assert his rights, so he was compensated—through his mother, of course. Emily was given a substantial cash sum to keep her son quiet and amenable."

Gertrude spoke quietly. "Are you trying to humiliate me?" She was tracing little patterns on the table-top in spilt coffee.

"No. I'm sure that you have had more than your share of humiliation, but I do intend to get at the truth."

She looked at him steadily for some time before speaking, then she said, "I was nineteen at the time—the same age as Esther is now, but there was no real comparison! I had had virtually no contact with boys other than with my brothers and Morley Newcombe. My parents were probably fond of me, but in the same way as they might have been of a pet cat; I was cosseted and protected and forbidden to grow up." She was staring at her coffee mug, turning it round with the tips of her fingers. "Well, there came a time when I was ripe for seduction, and I was seduced—by an expert—a natural."

Wycliffe said, "Isn't it surprising that your parents, so anxious to protect you, let you associate with Newcombe? I gather that he was already known as a girl-chaser."

She laughed briefly. "I knew nothing about that and I doubt if my parents did. As far as they were concerned the Newcombes were servants—and therefore *safe.*" She paused and her eyes took on a faraway look. "Ashill was another world then; sometimes I can hardly believe it was real. The uproar when they discovered that I was pregnant! And when they were eventually persuaded that the father was Morley Newcombe!

"Of course, my parents, Ruby Price and the priest went into conference. There could be no question of abortion but, in the end, they worked out the perfect solution; everything for the best. By marrying me, Frank bought his way into the firm and the family; Esther had a reputable father; I became respectable again, and Beales' Stores acquired a first-class businessman as a family property."

After an interval Wycliffe said, "Does Esther know?"

"I've never told her, but she knows—I'm quite sure of that."

"Shouldn't you have told her?"

She made an irritable movement. "Of course I should have told her! But in this family we never talk about anything that matters; we live on the surface and try not to think about what is underneath."

Unselfconsciously Wycliffe began to fill his pipe as he would have done in his kitchen at home. Gertrude felt the outside of her untouched mug of coffee and, finding it cold, pushed it away.

"I should have divorced him years ago but I am trapped. If I divorced him, what should I have? Can't you see that he is far more necessary to the family than I am? They wouldn't risk losing Frank."

Wycliffe changed the subject. "Esther seems a very self-reliant young woman."

"I suppose one could say that she has to be."

"And very protective towards Edward."

"She recognizes another victim."

"Victim?"

"Of this house—this family!" Her voice trembled, then broke; she slumped down with her arms on the table and her head in her arms and wept. Wycliffe was moved. He got up and went round the table to stand at her side, helpless.

The weeping turned to sobs and the sobs eventually subsided; she lifted her head, her face flushed and creased, her eyes swollen. She made no apology but said with a kind of satisfaction which seemed to invite and acknowledge his complicity, "That's the first time I've been able to do that in many years."

The atmosphere in the kitchen had become intimate; time for a middle-aged policeman to make a tactical withdrawal. He said, "Try not to worry."

It was a fatuous remark and she smiled up at him, blinking her reddened eyelids. "I'll be all right."

She came with him to the door and watched him down the steps. With little sleep and no breakfast he felt cold inside; uneasy too, as one who had come within shouting distance of making a fool of himself.

"I'll keep you informed."

Had Vicary cleared out? It seemed inconceivable that a man responsible for two murders should be scared off while there was still not a shred of real evidence against him. Incredible too, that he should not have used his car, at least on the first leg of his get-away.

Wycliffe told himself, "Find out where he spends Friday evenings —in particular, where he spent this one."

He had asked Gertrude, "Do you think there is a woman?" and Gertrude had answered, "I'd be very surprised." Another time she had said, "Frank is system personified, his whole life is run to a schedule." But even if Gertrude saw herself as a sex-starved woman it did not necessarily mean that Vicary was a eunuch. Certainly he was not the sort to complicate his life with any romantic involvement; it was unlikely that he had a Veronica tucked away; more likely there was a business arrangement, efficiently stage-managed, something more subtle than a short-time with a tenner on the mantelpiece though with the same lack of commitment.

But where?

In the yard Sergeant Smith, P.C. Miller and a little dark man in overalls were standing round Vicary's car.

Smith was at his most dour. "This is Mr. Smerdon who runs the garage on the Newton road, sir. Vicary is one of his customers."

The little man, who looked like Adolf Hitler and obviously knew it, chipped in. "He has a charge account for petrol and he's a fanatic about economy." When my chap fills his tank he sets the trip meter back to zero so that he can check the performance." Smerdon was smoking a tiny black cheroot which wiggled up and down as he spoke.

"When was he last in?"

"Yesterday evening between half past five and six. My boy was off so I served him myself. I asked him if he was going to the fair and got a dusty answer; he's not a chatty sort of man. What do you think has happened to him, Superintendent?"

"I've no more idea than you have."

Smith cut in. "The trip meter is reading five point two miles and the tank is still as good as full, so he can't have gone far." Smith turned his morose gaze on P.C. Miller. "Miller has a notion about where he might have gone."

Miller had a cautious man's aversion to sticking his neck out but he had no option. "It's just that five miles is about the distance from the garage to Biscombe and back here. Biscombe is a little place a couple of miles down the valley."

"So?"

"Well, sir, it occurred to me that Vicary might be a visitor at Biscombe Manor. I mean, it's possible he spent his Friday evenings there."

"Why? Is it an hotel or something?"

"No, sir. A few years back it was leased to a chap called Lyne, a retired property dealer from London. He came down here with his wife and daughter; his wife has left him, but his daughter is still there and I hear that she's well in with the horsey set."

"Why should Vicary go there, do you think?"

Miller frowned. This was getting too specific. "I don't know that he did, sir, but I've heard that Lyne has several friends among businessmen who live round here and I thought Vicary might be one of them. I often see cars in Lyne's drive of an evening."

Wycliffe nodded. "It sounds promising." He turned to Smith. "Did anything about the car strike you as unusual?"

Smith shook his grey head. "Nothing. There's no sign that anybody drove it but the owner—his prints are everywhere; and there are no indications of any violence. In my view Vicary drove his car home and parked it as usual. What happened after that . . ."

What happened after that was the crunch question.

Wycliffe, on the point of telephoning Biscombe Manor, changed his mind. If, by any chance, the man Lyne was involved in Vicary's disappearance there was an obvious risk in telephoning. He decided to go there himself.

He picked up his car from the Green and drove down South Street to the Newton road. Almost opposite the junction a finger-post pointed along a narrow lane: BISCOMBE 2 MILES. The lane roughly followed the course of a stream in a gentle switchback, until topping one rise, he was looking down on a hamlet of a score or so houses. The stream, now almost a river, and moving more sedately, skirted the houses and meandered through the arches of a packhorse bridge which carried the road to the manor house on the opposite hill. The house itself, grey stone and slate, with steep gables, was backed by sombre pines against the high moor. The mists had thinned and a watery sunshine lit the valley in startling contrast with the inky-black clouds lying heavily on the face of the moor. Wycliffe drove through the seemingly deserted village, over the pack-horse bridge (maximum width six feet) and up the hill to the house. He left his car in the drive and went up the steps of a Victorian Gothic porch to a front door studded with nails and decorated with all the wrought-iron trimmings.

His ring was answered by Lyne himself, a wiry little cockney who, despite his expensive tweeds, would have looked more at home behind a stall on the Portobello Road.

Wycliffe introduced himself and Lyne's eyes narrowed. "Chief Super! What's this about then?" He remembered his manners. "At any rate whatever it is you can tell me better inside." He led the way into a large drawing-room which looked like a lounge bar in an up-market pub. "Drink? I've got a nice drop of scotch sent me by a friend . . ."

Wycliffe excused himself. "I wanted to ask you if Frank Vicary of Ashill was here last night."

Lyne looked surprised. "Frankie? What's he been up to then? In any case, why don't you ask him?"

"Because we can't find him, Mr. Lyne. His car is back at Ashill but there's no sign of the man himself."

"Well I'll be damned!" Lyne poured whisky from a crystal decanter into a matching glass. "Sure you won't change your mind? I never drink when I'm here alone, but you being here . . ." He chuckled. "It'd be a pity to pass up the chance." He sipped the neat spirit. "Well, Frankie was here last night like every other Friday— but a chief super don't come looking for any Charlie who happens to stay out all night; is this about the Washford murders?"

"That's what I'm trying to find out, Mr. Lyne. What does Vicary do when he comes here?"

"Do? He does the same as the rest of us—we play nap."

"Nap?"

Lyne laughed. "It's a good game—English poker. And the way we play it's cut-throat."

"Big stakes?"

"Far from it! Never more than a few pounds change hands in a night but you'd think we was playing for the Crown jewels and Frankie is the keenest of the lot."

"Who else was here last night?"

"The usual Friday night set. Apart from Frankie and me there was Ernie Pemberton, a retired estate agent from Noseworthy, and Billy Norris who used to run a night-club in Torquay—Billy is retired too and lives a mile or so down the valley—another fish out of water." Lyne looked out of the window where the sunlight was still struggling through the mists in a ready-made watercolour. "Biggest mistake of my life, coming to a place where there's nothing to do but die. If it wasn't for my girl I'd flog the bloody lease and get back to the smoke."

"What time did Vicary leave?"

"About half-eleven; he never stays late—afraid of missing the early worm. A keen lad, our Frankie."

"He comes here every Friday night to play nap—is that it?"

"What else? A game of cards, a drink or two, and a chat."

"No women?"

Lyne laughed. "You think I run a brothel on the side? It's an idea —liven the place up a bit but I don't think it would appeal to Frankie. Seriously though, no women."

"What sort of a chap is Vicary?"

Lyne shook his head. "That's asking." He emptied his glass and put it down. "I'm no head-shrinker."

"But you know men; you've had to if I've got the measure of you."

Lyne grinned. "You're a persuasive bugger, I'll give you that. All right! I'd say Frankie is a born fighter who can never win."

"A very odd description of a successful businessman."

"You think so? I wouldn't say that. Some people—a lot maybe, never win if there's nobody there to cheer."

"You think he needs someone to tell him what a clever bloke he is?"

Lyne gave him an odd look. "Why not? We're all human. Frankie himself doesn't say much but from what I've heard elsewhere the Beales are a rum crowd. He hits it off with the old man because he knows how to make the tills sing, but aside from that . . . One of the brothers is as thick as two short planks and the other seems to be bonkers. As for Frankie's wife . . . Lyne tilted his elbow. "Like me, she's too fond of the firewater but from what I hear she don't wait for visitors."

"Last night, did he seem much as usual?"

"He was under the weather. I went out with him to his car and we chatted for a minute or two before he drove off. I could tell he was worried about the killings." Lyne paused then added, "Last night Frankie was a very worried man."

Wycliffe thanked him. "I'll send someone along to take your statement."

"Anytime! I'm always glad of somebody to talk to in this mausoleum. And if, any night, you feel like a game of cards and a drink, you know where to come."

He stood on the steps and watched Wycliffe drive off.

Wycliffe now knew where Vicary went on Friday evenings and much good it did him. He was still not sure whether he was looking for a fugitive or a victim though it seemed unlikely that a man would spend a social evening with friends before making a bolt for it.

He drove back to Washford and parked on the Green. Kersey was in the van and they brought each other up to date.

"Curnow talked to Charlie Alford—he had to prod him a bit by dangling a charge of exhibitionism. Alford admitted sending you the note—more out of spite against the Beales than anything else. He found out about Edward's father by chance—a relative of his wife in the Met—and he couldn't resist making something of it. Perhaps more important, he told Curnow that not long after his mother died, Newcombe had said, 'She had money. I know the old bitch had money and I know where she got it, but I can't bloody well find out what she done with it.' And another time, still talking about the money, he said, 'Anyway, I reckon there's more where that come from.' "

"Anything else?"

"Just that Moss, who was on obo last night in South Street, says the gates were open when Vicary came back and he drove straight in, but a minute or so later he came to shut the gates and Moss saw him quite clearly."

Wycliffe said, "You've got a search team out?"

"They've been at it for some time. Perhaps there's something for them to find."

Wycliffe was restless. He left the van and walked through the main gates of Ashill, round the house and across the lawn. The mists had closed in again, clammily damp, though not unpleasant, for the moisture in the air caught and held the tangy smells of the peaty soil and of the plants which grew in it. He needed time to think. It occurred to him that Vicary might have felt the same—coming back from Biscombe he might have felt the need of time to adjust before returning to the claustrophobic atmosphere of Ashill and to the fresh tensions generated by the murders. Wasn't it quite possible that he had taken a midnight stroll in the grounds? Last night at that time it could have been very pleasant—a fine night, moonshine, the glare from the fair, the babel of music and voices, hoots and cries. . . . But if he had taken such a stroll, what had happened to him?

There was, of course, another possibility, that Vicary was the killer and, convinced that he had no chance of getting away with it, he had chosen to take his own life. But nothing he had heard of the man suggested that he would give in so easily.

He reached the ivy-covered wall at the back of Quarry House and peered through the slatted gate into the dripping, deserted garden. He made a mental note to find out whether Nicholas had been visiting there the night before. He continued walking through the trees to the little pavilion above the fall and it was as he was ascending the zigzag path that he looked down and saw, by the margin of the pool, four men standing around a body which was sprawled on the ground.

Vicary had been found.

They had found him in the shallow, slack water near the fall, along with a mass of other debris which had been caught up and swept aside by the turbulence. The searchers had dragged the body ashore and now it lay on the muddy shingle, still within reach of the spray from the fall. Wycliffe looked down at the small crumpled figure. Vicary wore a light-grey pin-stripe with grey-suede shoes, silk shirt and tie to match; all sodden now, so that water seeped from them. His face was devoid of colour but seemed to be smiling; his wide, thin-lipped mouth was widened still further in a sardonic grin.

One of the men said, "We radioed the van, sir. Mr. Kersey is on his way."

Vicary had not drowned. Like the others he had been shot through the head though the wound of entry was not immediately obvious. It was low down, well behind the ear, a neat hole, as though a pencil had been pressed in. The wound of exit was less discreet, the bullet had blasted its way out of the temporal region on the other side of the skull.

Wycliffe stooped down and felt the oddly flexed limbs to satisfy himself that rigor was still present. As he did so he noticed that the dead man's wallet was on the point of slipping out of the inside breast pocket of his jacket and he picked it up.

A third violent death in less than a week and suicide was out. Apart from the circumstances in which the body had been found, the position of the wound of entry made it highly improbable, and the nature of the wound meant that the gun had been discharged at some distance—not far, but outside the practical range of suicide.

Only yesterday he had begun to realize the possible strength of a case against Vicary, now Vicary was dead. He felt a heavy responsibility; almost as though the man had died as a direct result of his suspicion—which was absurd. All the same . . . Joyce had said to him: "You think you've found out something but you could still get it wrong." Now her words had a prophetic ring.

Kersey arrived. A master of platitude in moments of high drama, he said, "This is getting to be a habit!"

"What do you make of it?"

Kersey took his time. "It seems pretty obvious that he was shot and pushed in the water afterwards."

Wycliffe said, "Rigor is still present and the limbs are flexed as you see. I doubt if they set that way while supported in the water."

"You think he was already stiff when he went in?"

"It looks that way to me."

"But that would mean an interval of several hours between the shooting and the time he went into the water."

Wycliffe changed the subject. "We shall have to leave that to Franks. Meantime, we agree that he wasn't shot in the water, so where?"

Kersey ran a hand through his thinning hair and looked at the flotsam trapped in the shallows where the body had been found, then up the gleaming face of the fall. "I suppose that stuff came from up there by the quick way; perhaps he did too."

By radio, and for the third time in six days, Wycliffe set in motion the machinery of a murder inquiry.

To make access easier and to avoid having to carry the body up the steep slope by the fall, the four searchers were put to work clearing a way through the shrubbery to the lane, where there was a decaying wooden door which had not been opened for a generation at least.

Wycliffe brooded over the body. It lay on its back as it had been dragged from the water, legs and arms flexed in a bizarre position like a badly trussed turkey, a posture which only made sense if the body was face down. When Vicary was shot he must have collapsed face down, arms and legs somewhat retracted; rigor had set in and, hours later, the now rigid body had been dropped or pushed into the pool. If the shooting had taken place soon after Vicary's return home, the body could have found its way into the water by six or seven in the morning, but not earlier.

Odd!

And there was something else; the fingers of the right hand were set in a holding position though the hand was empty.

"What do you make of that hand?"

Kersey screwed up his lips. "Not much; it looks as though he might have been holding something when rigor set in."

Wycliffe said, "If I'm not here when Smith comes make sure he gets a shot of that hand and ask Franks what he makes of it."

Wycliffe was still holding the dead man's wallet—pigskin, darkened by immersion. He opened it: several sodden five-pound notes and a couple of singles; driving licence; cheque cards, and a car insurance certificate. In an inside pocket where the water had not penetrated to the same extent he found a folded sheet of writing paper which turned out to be a handwritten letter. The writing was large, round and schoolgirlish and he thought he recognized it before he saw the signature—Ruby Price.

Dear Frank,   Friday.

I am no longer welcome at the house and, as I never go into the city, I thought it best to write. I am sending this to your office and it is for you to decide whether or not you show it to G. Yesterday I had a visit from N. At first I thought he was drunk because he talked about his rights as a parent! Then he went on to say that now his mother is dead he is determined to have what he claims to be "his due." He talked about "having the law on some people" and said that if it came to that I would have to tell the truth on oath. Of course I know that this is mostly big talk but he is out to make trouble and I think he's shrewd enough to see that he can do it without bringing in the law. He said he was thinking of having a word with G. and then, if necessary, with the girl. I told him what I thought of him in no uncertain terms but I'm worried on behalf of the family and for dear R's sake.

With kind regards,
Ruby Price.

Wycliffe noted that Ruby had not been in any great hurry to pass on news of the visit. He handed the letter to Kersey.

Kersey read it and shook his head. "It seems a hell of a lot of sweat about an illegitimate kid twenty years after."

Wycliffe left him to cope with the pathologist and the removal of the body. He climbed the steep path to the pavilion at the head of the fall, opened the red-painted door and stepped inside.

As before the little room looked neglected, dusty and unused; everywhere there were signs of mouldering damp. Between worn and patternless rugs, floor-boards were visible and there were narrow gaps through which he could glimpse the racing water below. One wall was taken up with cupboards; there were a large, oblong table, three or four wicker chairs with damp, faded cushions and a sofa.

He looked for any signs that the shooting had taken place there but found nothing more suggestive than a pale rectangular patch on the floor where it seemed a rug had been removed. One certain change since his last visit, the cupboard doors had been shut, now they stood open. Some of the shelves were stacked with old magazines and books which were losing their spines; others held board games, packs of cards, anonymous boxes of all sizes, a cheap camera, table tennis bats. . . . In one of the cupboards a section of the bottom shelf had been removed exposing a cavity in the masonry—the sort of secret hidey-hole children love—and in the cavity he could see the end of a cardboard box which was far too clean to have been there long. He lifted it out and found a smaller, stouter one below it. The smaller box carried a Fiocchi label and contained thirteen nine-millimetre cartridges. The other box was something of a lucky dip—medals, ribbons, regimental cap badges, shoulder flashes . . . Nicholas's souvenirs.

He looked into the cavity again and felt round to make sure but there was no pistol.

It seemed likely that Vicary had been shot in the pavilion and later—much later—his body had been dragged on to the veranda and tumbled over the balustrade. His men would search for the cartridge-case and the bullet, they would crawl over the floor and minutely inspect the veranda and balustrade; they would end up with several little polyethylene bags neatly labelled, and this would be proof.

He went out on to the veranda. Mist blotted out the valley; moisture condensed on every surface and dripped from the eaves of the little building. Very different from the night before when Vicary had parked his car in the yard and been cajoled or coerced into trailing across the lawn and through the trees to the pavilion. At that time the fair was lighting up the sky over Ashill, the night was clear and there was a moon.

Wycliffe left the pavilion and walked on through the trees to the back of Quarry House. He let himself into the garden and walked up the path to the back door. Through the window he could see into the kitchen where the two sisters were seated at table, eating their lunch.

It was Veronica who came to the door.

Wycliffe said, "I would like to talk to you and your sister."

Veronica stretched her lean, freckled neck like a bird in aggressive display, but something in his manner must have checked her for she stood aside to let him in.

In the kitchen Rose got up from the table with a nervous smile. "We eat in here at midday, it hardly seems worth carrying everything into the dining-room."

Veronica said, "I hardly think the superintendent is interested in our domestic arrangements, Rose." She stood by the table without inviting him to sit down.

"Last night, at about midnight, Frank Vicary was shot dead in the little house over the fall."

He cut short the exclamations of shocked concern. "Presumably you were here last night at that time?"

Veronica said, "We must have been preparing for bed."

"You heard nothing—no shot?"

"There was so much noise from the fair it would have been difficult to hear anything; they went on until one o'clock."

"Before you went to bed, did you go into your back garden at all?"

Rose looked at Veronica, who seemed slightly self-conscious. She said, "I was in the garden briefly, that was probably a few minutes before midnight."

On their two plates, lettuce leaves were growing soggy in the liquid which drained from little pink chunks of tinned salmon. If this was typical of Quarry House cuisine, Nicholas was not being wooed through his stomach.

"Was Captain Beale here last night?"

"He was." Very stiff.

"And you were seeing him off?"

"Captain Beale comes and goes by the back gate because it is obviously more convenient for him. As we like to lock the gate at night, I go down the garden with him."

"Were you in the garden for any length of time?"

"A few minutes—perhaps six or seven."

"Before or after Captain Beale left?"

She coloured like a young girl. "Before."

"Presumably you were both near the gate?"

"Fairly near."

"In those few minutes did anything strike you as unusual or odd—did you hear or see anything out of the ordinary? Other than the fair, of course."

She was all set for a denial but then her expression changed.

Wycliffe said, "I can see that there was something—what was it?"

She shrugged. "It was really nothing at all; I don't know why I remembered it. I thought I heard footsteps—somebody hurrying, passing the gate—I had my back to it."

"And?"

"I happened to mention it to Captain Beale because I know they are concerned about night prowlers on the estate but he said he hadn't noticed anything."

"Did Captain Beale carry a torch?"

"He always carries one when he comes here in the evening but it wasn't needed last night, with the moon and the lights from the fair it was like day."

"How was he dressed?"

This was too much for Veronica. "Really, Mr. Wycliffe, I think you should ask him such a question."

"But I'm asking you."

Rose sat as though transfixed; this was not the man she had chatted to so amiably in the churchyard.

"He wore a green cardigan and cavalry twill trousers."

"No jacket or coat?"

"No."

"And he carried nothing but a torch?"

"That is correct."

"Does he usually stay until midnight?"

Veronica flushed but she answered. "He usually leaves at about half past ten but last night there was a concert on the radio which we particularly wanted to hear."

Wycliffe left the sisters to their tinned salmon and, on his way to Ashill, he brooded on oddities. "If a case has a number of unusual features the chances are they are related." A truth handed down from on high during his training days and duly recorded in his notebook. Well, there were odd features here. The near-coincidence between the time at which Nicholas left his Veronica and the time of the shooting; the fact that he was much later leaving than usual; the fact that though the army souvenirs and ammunition had turned up—more or less exhibited—the pistol was still missing; the fact that Vicary had, apparently gone to the pavilion instead of to bed; that he had been shot, and hours later tumbled into the pool; that his hand was curiously flexed. And one other fact—that Nicholas was already out when Wycliffe arrived at Ashill that morning.

The links if they existed were too tenuous for a plodding policeman who always had difficulty with sustained logical thought.

He arrived in the coach-house yard and climbed the steps to the flat. Gertrude answered the door and took his coat. While they were still in the hall he said, "I'm afraid it's bad news."

"Tell me."

"I'm sorry to say that your husband is dead."

They moved into the drawing-room and she pointed, mechanically, to a chair but they remained standing. She walked over to the window.

Wycliffe said, "He was shot through the head."

It was some while before she asked, "Would he have suffered much pain? He was a child about pain."

"Death must have been instantaneous."

The gloom outside seemed to drain what little colour there was from the room, leaving sombre greys, and as Gertrude stood by the window he could only see her form in silhouette.

She spoke in a low voice, her manner reflective. "It shows how little one can know of another person. I would never have believed him capable—"

"Capable of what?"

She turned to face him in apparent surprise. "Of doing what he must have done and then taking his own life."

"He didn't kill himself."

"I thought you said—"

"I said that he had been found shot—shot by someone, murdered like the others."

She looked at him, wide-eyed, fearful, "But you found the gun?"
"No."

She moved to the nearest chair and dropped into it; she seemed profoundly shocked. "Then it isn't over! I could see yesterday that you thought Frank . . . that you suspected him." She was twisting her hands together and staring at him with frightened eyes. "I found it difficult to believe; I didn't think he was capable of such violence, but I *wanted* you to be right—I *wanted* it to be Frank. . . . When you told me that he was dead I must confess I thought, 'It's over! At least it's over!' "

"Did you?" The words came softly and he was gazing at her with an intensity of which he himself was unaware. He had not intended to speak his question aloud; in fact he had been asking himself whether she was genuinely distressed or whether it was an act.

She said, "Why are you looking at me like that? Are you trying to frighten me? There's no need. God! I'm frightened enough already. Because it isn't over and you will go on and on until . . ."

There was hysteria in her voice. She reached for a cigarette from a box on the table, lit it, inhaled and blew out a cloud of smoke.

Wycliffe said, speaking very quietly. "Your husband was shot; then, much later, his body was pushed into the pool."

"In the pool? You found him in the pool? Why are you saying this? You must have a reason, or is it just to torment me?" She was flushed and her hands trembled so that she had difficulty in placing the cigarette between her lips.

"I am telling you what actually happened."

She was staring at him fixedly but he could see that she had accepted what he said and was trying desperately to fit it in with whatever pattern her thoughts presented. "But if someone did that to him—I mean, if they shifted his body, he still might have killed himself."

"No. The position and the nature of the wound rule out suicide."

She had made a great effort of self-control and when she spoke again her voice was calmer but also harder. "Have you found out where he went last night?"

"To Biscombe Manor, where he spent every Friday evening."

"Not with a woman."

"No, he went there to play cards with a few friends."

She nodded. "That's more like it!" Suddenly she was aggressive, almost vicious; she crushed out her half-smoked cigarette. "I knew that there was no woman—he was impotent, that's why he had to be such a big man in the business."

She was silent for a while, the knuckles of one hand pressed to her lips. "You're quite sure it couldn't have been suicide? The gun could have been taken from his hand as they put him in the water—"

"Suicide is out of the question."

It was chilly and he felt oddly oppressed in this large, anonymous room where it was easy to believe that nothing had ever happened which people could look back on with pleasure or warmth. A room that was a mere backdrop for episodes rather than a place where someone had lived.

"When did you last see Newcombe?"

The question took her by surprise and she hesitated. "See him? I don't know. . . . A long time ago." She added after a pause, "Over the years I've done my best not to see him."

"Are you sure that you haven't spoken to him recently?"

She moved irritably. "What is the good of asking me questions if you don't believe what I say?"

He took Ruby's letter from his pocket and handed it to her. "I found this in your husband's wallet."

She took the letter and read it through with obvious anxiety, then she looked at him, "When did he get this?"

"Presumably at his office on Saturday."

She was very pale. "I've never seen it before; I didn't even know of its existence."

"And you still say that Newcombe hasn't been to see you?"

She seemed deeply preoccupied. "I've told you!"

"On Sunday your husband went to see Newcombe—what happened then?"

She burst out, "You ask me? I didn't even know that he'd been until after Newcombe was dead. He told me nothing—nothing ever!"

"And now Newcombe, Ruby Price and your husband have all been murdered."

She looked at him once more with scared eyes. "What are you trying to say?"

"Only that I am searching for a motive—a motive strong enough to account for the killing of three people."

"I—" She broke off at the sound of the front door opening and of someone in the hall. "That will be Esther; she hasn't been to work today."

Esther came in wearing jeans and a denim jacket. Little globules of moisture were trapped in her hair; she looked desperately tired.

"You've been out?"

The girl did not answer her mother but spoke to Wycliffe. "So you've found him."

Gertrude said, "Your father's body was found in the pool, he had been shot through the head."

"I know." But she continued to address Wycliffe, "He didn't do it himself?"

"No."

The girl remained where she was for a moment, irresolute, then she turned in a deliberate way and left the room.

Gertrude said, "She's off to find Edward; I'm no use to her."

"Will you break the news to your father?"

"I suppose I must."

"I'll see myself out." He felt sure that her need for a stiff drink was all but overwhelming.

Esther had not gone in search of Edward, she was waiting for Wycliffe in the hall. She pushed open one of the doors and beckoned him in. It was her bedroom, a plainly furnished little room, cheerless as a nun's cell.

"Will she be all right?"

Wycliffe preferred not to answer.

"What are you going to do?"

Her tiredness bordered on exhaustion; her movements were slow and the dark rings under her eyes were like bruises.

Again Wycliffe said nothing and she went on, "It's like a horrible nightmare, like being in a room with the walls closing in. . . . I saw your men in the pavilion, is it right that he was shot there?"

"I think so."

"But his body was found in the pool."

"Yes, we think it was tumbled over the balustrade."

She put her hand to her mouth in a curiously childish gesture. "Mother couldn't have done that! She has a back injury—she couldn't possibly . . ."

She looked at him, more frightened than ever, realizing that by her very denial she had brought into the open the stark possibility of her mother's guilt, and now, there it was, pinned out between them like a specimen for inspection.

"Why don't you sit down?"

Obediently she sat on the bottom of her bed, upright and tense.

"How long have you known that Frank Vicary was not your real father?"

She swept back her hair with both hands. "It's hard to say; it gradually dawned on me that our family wasn't quite right, and when I was a bit older I overheard things. I realized that Mother had had a lover before she was married and that I was the result." She smiled briefly. "I thought it was romantic until I found out who her lover had been."

"When was that?"

"I must have been thirteen."

"Who told you?"

"Ruby Price—with a lot of satisfaction. I know it wasn't long after Granny Beale died, she wouldn't have dared before."

"You didn't like Ruby?"

She considered the question. "It was mutual. I wouldn't call her 'Auntie' and that sort of thing, so she always pretended to forget my name and called me 'girl.' . . . No, I didn't like her at all. She had a way of talking—always hinting at what she could say if she chose." She broke off, then added, "I know Teddy feels differently about her."

Wycliffe said, "Last night you went to the fair and you came back at about a quarter to ten; what did you do after that?"

She frowned. "Nothing really. Mother was in the drawing-room—"

"Did you speak to her?"

"No, the television was on and she was asleep in her chair. I came in here and lay on the bed reading until about half past eleven, then I decided to make myself something to drink before going to bed properly. I went into the kitchen, but it occurred to me that Mother might like something too, so I went to ask her, but she was fast asleep. I switched off the television and left her, that's the best thing to do when she is like that."

An alibi?

Chapter Eight

Although leaden clouds had rolled down from the moor to engulf the village in a moist gloom, it was still not raining. Wycliffe joined Kersey in the police caravan where young Dixon was duty officer and two other D.C.s pecked away at typewriters.

Kersey said, "I've had a call from Radford of *The News;* it seems his colleagues have pushed off for the weekend and left him holding the baby. He's heard a rumour and I promised him a statement this afternoon but he's not too bothered. His own paper doesn't come out again till Monday and over the weekend, local TV and radio are only interested in balls of different shapes and sizes, kicked, hit, thrown or poked."

"What's happened down below?"

"Franks has been and gone; he agrees with you—definitely not suicide, an interval of several hours between the shooting and the body going into the water, and he admits that the right hand could have held a gun which was forcibly removed after rigor had set in. They've taken the body away and Smith has gone back to headquarters to work on his stuff. Among other things he's taken fibres from the stonework of the balustrade which might have come from Vicary's clothing."

"Good! Let's see if we can get something to eat."

The village seemed deserted and the fun-fair, due for a final fling that evening, was shrouded in dripping canvas. But the inn wasn't short of customers though they were anything but lively. They sat in silence, sipping their beer and contemplating the table-tops. The two policemen were received with indifference.

But Blatchford was the same as ever. "They're always like this on the day after. Most of 'em had a skinful last night and they need time to get over it." He lowered his voice, "They're saying that Vicary shot himself."

Wycliffe took refuge in the Irish, "Are they now!"

"I saw your chaps buzzing around just now and I wondered . . ."

They shared the railed-off part of the bar with a young unisex couple of would-be walkers who, as they ate, kept an anxious eye on the window and the menacing clouds.

Dora served them with hot pasties and Wycliffe watched with gloomy fascination while Kersey opened his and filled it with tomato ketchup. Afterwards they had treacle pudding with clotted cream, a meal which would not have gained Helen's seal of approval.

At a quarter to two, when they returned to the van, the wind was rising, stirring the limp flags and rustling through the beech trees.

"I want you to put a man in the entrance hall at the house."

"Am I allowed to ask why?"

Wycliffe was vague. "It will raise the temperature a bit and he might be useful."

The church clock was chiming the hour when Wycliffe crossed to the house and let himself in by the front door without ringing the bell. There was no one about so he hung his coat and hat in the little cloakroom. As he turned down the L-shaped passage he all but ran into Joyce. She looked at him, startled, but no longer aggressive.

"Mr. Simon's been asking for you, he would like to see you in his room—he's in there with Mr. Maurice and Miss Gertrude."

"Where are the others?"

"Mr. Nicholas is in the library, Mrs. Naomi is upstairs, resting."

"What about Edward and Esther?"

"They're up in his studio. He usually goes to Torquay on Saturdays where he sells his pictures but I heard him on the phone, putting it off." She went on, "They've none of them had any lunch but I took round bowls of soup."

The little button eyes were fearful. "When is it all going to end?"

"Soon."

He went along the passage. Simon's door was partly open and Maurice was speaking on the telephone, his voice high-pitched, domineering and querulous.

"I know quite well that there are problems but you will have to cope. . . . Definitely not!" The receiver was replaced with a clatter.

Wycliffe went in and stood just inside the door. Simon was seated at his desk and Maurice, feathers ruffled, stood beside him. Gertrude was seated in a wing-chair, her handbag in her lap, like a visitor.

The old man passed a thin hand over his white hair. "This is a great blow, Mr. Wycliffe. This morning I was very much afraid, but I hoped—"

Maurice said in his most sententious voice, "It is a great tragedy!"

Simon made a sudden, vicious movement which scattered the papers on his desk. "Of course it's a tragedy, you fool! How much of a tragedy you'll find out in the coming months, you and your precious wife!"

Maurice flushed but said nothing. Wycliffe could not see Gertrude's reaction as she had her back to him. The burst of temper had taken it out of the old man; spots of colour appeared on his pale cheeks and his hands were trembling. He made an effort at composure. "I'm sorry, Mr. Wycliffe, but what has happened has been a very great shock. I didn't believe it could come to that. There are things I must tell you . . ."

Quite suddenly Wycliffe had had enough of the Beale treatment, as much as he could take. He said, "I doubt if there is anything you can tell me now, Mr. Beale, that would be of use. Earlier it might have been different." He turned towards the door. "I must ask you all to remain in the house for the time being."

It did no good, but he felt better.

As he came out of Simon's room he saw Potter's massive bulk stationed in the hall looking useful, like a spare tyre.

Nicholas was seated at his desk, which was littered with maps, photostats of documents, historical journals, and two large, leatherbound volumes with gilded spines. The bowl of soup Joyce had brought stood untouched and congealing amid the rest.

Nicholas's pale features accorded Wycliffe a minimum of acknowledgement and he was left to find a chair for himself and to place it near the desk. As he did so the rain came, lashing against the windows, and across the lawn the trees cowered under a wild sky. Twigs in new leaf were torn off to come bowling across the grass like phantom hoops.

"I suppose you've heard that your brother-in-law's body has been found in the pool?"

Nicholas said nothing but his eyes seemed to assent.

"He was shot in the pavilion at about midnight last night and several hours later his body was dragged out and hoisted over the balustrade."

Nicholas remained motionless, his large hands clasped lightly together on the desk. His face was expressionless but a persistent tic affected one corner of his mouth.

"Last night you left Quarry House at about midnight and, when I arrived here this morning, you had already gone out." Wycliffe paused for this to sink in then, casually, he said, "What did you do with the gun? Either you threw it into the pool or you still have it. My guess is that you kept it."

The two men sat on opposite sides of the desk; Wycliffe, apparently relaxed; Nicholas, despite his superficial calm, drawn and pale, a man near the end of his tether. He remained silent for a long time and Wycliffe made no move to hurry him.

At last he spoke, "You are quite right; there is no point in prolonging this." With slow, deliberate movements he opened a drawer of his desk, lifted out the pistol and laid it on the desk.

Wycliffe said, "When did you get it back?"

Nicholas's eyes registered alarm. "It has never been out of my possession. Your experts will tell you that this is the gun used in the three murders and it has never been out of my hands. I take full responsibility for what I have done."

Wycliffe spoke in a tired voice as though reviewing events whose significance was already in the past. "Last night, while you were still in the garden at Quarry House, you saw someone hurry by the gate. Miss Gould heard the footsteps but she had her back to the gate and did not see who it was."

Nicholas would have interrupted but Wycliffe cut him off. "There is no need to say anything at the moment; let me finish. As I say I am quite sure that you saw and recognized someone and that someone was the killer. I am not sure whether or not you were seen."

The only perceptible response from Nicholas was a tightening of the jaw muscles; a tic still tugged at one corner of his mouth. Wycliffe went on: "It was only this morning, when you heard that Vicary had not returned you found his car in the yard, that you became worried; you realized the possible significance of what you had seen and you went out to check. You found Vicary's body in the pavilion; he had been shot through the head and, in his right hand, he held your gun—the Beretta. The implication was suicide but you knew too much about firearms to be taken in and you knew that the police would not be either."

Nicholas could control himself no longer; he burst out, "This is intolerable! I have volunteered a formal statement at a police station—"

But for once, Wycliffe showed a flash of temper. He slammed the desk with the flat of his hand. "What you have volunteered to do is to tell me more lies! Since last Monday I have been lied to by every member of your family. Sometimes the lying has had a more or less creditable motive but more often it has been naked self-interest or concern for the Beale image. Not once has anybody shown the slightest concern for the victims—not even for the one who was a member of the family."

Wycliffe got to his feet and went to the window where he stood, watching the rain which blotted out the whole landscape.

"When you found your brother-in-law's body your first reaction was to delay its discovery by anyone else. You took your pistol from his hand, dragged the body to the veranda and toppled it over the fall. You thought it would sink in the fresh water and remain submerged for several days. You would have time to think. Fortunately the body was caught by the turbulence and swept into the shallows."

He stopped speaking but remained looking out of the window with his back to Nicholas. For a time there was only the sound of the rain beating against the windows then Wycliffe said, "The point is that you were ready if necessary to take the responsibility for three murders. I think there are only two people for whom you might be prepared to do that—your sister and your niece."

Nicholas reacted angrily. "My sister and my niece have nothing whatever to do with this! I demand to be taken to a police station where I can make a formal statement—a confession or whatever you like to call it."

It was at this point that Wycliffe saw Gertrude; Gertrude wearing a green cape and hood with rubber boots, hurrying across the lawn, leaning against the wind and rain.

Ignoring Nicholas, Wycliffe went to the door and called out, "Potter!"

Potter arrived at the double. Wycliffe pointed to the gun. "I'm leaving you to get this to Mr. Kersey. I want it sent for ballistics tests—you know what to do?"

"Yes, sir."

Leaving Nicholas without a word, Wycliffe went into the hall, collected his mackintosh and hat from the cloakroom, and let himself out by the front door. A choked drain had caused a huge brown pool to spread over the gravel and he had to make a detour, but he rounded the house and set out across the lawn. Gertrude, of course, was nowhere to be seen but he thought he knew where to find her. The force of the wind abated as he reached the trees, only to increase again as he emerged at the pavilion, exposed to its full force.

He opened the little red door and went in. Gertrude was there, standing by the window, staring out at the storm. The torrential rain had swollen the stream and the roar of the fall beneath the little building seemed to threaten its very existence.

Without turning away from the window she said, "I wanted to come here; I thought it would be my last chance."

Wycliffe said nothing and she went on: "I realize that it's all over. When you left this morning I could see that there was no way out."

A long interval during which the roar of the water and the wind seemed to take possession of them, then she said, "I've always loved it here in this weather; you could be in the ark—water roaring underneath and pouring out of the sky; the rest of the world being washed away. . . . When we were young we used to spend a lot of time down here. It was a sort of club room and a refuge from the house. . . . If you look in the cupboards you'll find games, packs of cards and stacks of old books and magazines . . . there's a dartboard somewhere and we used to stretch a net across the table and play Ping-Pong. Maurice became quite expert—"

"Did Newcombe come here?"

"Oh yes, we were thoroughly democratic. He was the wizard of the dartboard." On the surface she was relaxed but her speech was jerky, the words coming in little bursts.

She turned away from the window, back into the room. "Of course it was later, after Nicholas had joined the army and Maurice was working in the firm, that we used to meet here."

"You mean you met Newcombe here regularly?"

"Oh yes, it was a real affair, not just a brief encounter." She smiled. "It lasted three months, until I discovered that I was pregnant." She looked down at the threadbare sofa which had once been upholstered in red velvet and patted it. *"La couche d'amour."*

"Were you in love with him?"

She laughed self-consciously. "What a question from a policeman! It was very romantic—on my side. He was my Noble Savage." She glanced up at Wycliffe and away again. "I had a very old-fashioned upbringing, Mr. Wycliffe—no television, very little radio and lots of more or less improving books. I was going to educate and refine him—do a Pygmalion . . . Absurd, wasn't it? A real little peasant, cunning and greedy, with a taste for honey and a way with stupid young girls."

She stood by the sofa, leaning against the arm. "Still, at the time I would have married him if they had let me. Who knows? It might have turned out better for both of us. Of course the committee wouldn't hear of it."

"The committee?"

"That's what we called them—they brought us up—my mother, Ruby Price and the priest."

"Not your father?"

"Father never interfered in what he called 'the domestic department'—that included his children until they were ripe to enter the firm. Of course it only worked with Maurice, but that was the theory.

"I tried to have a real conversation with Father once—after they knew I was pregnant, and he said, 'My dear girl! I can't possibly talk to you about such things—have a word with your mother or with Ruby Price.' This from a man who was going to bed with any woman who would slip off her pants for him . . ."

She was talking compulsively, a flood of words. Abruptly she changed the subject. "You were with Nicky—poor, dear Nicky. . . . When we were talking this morning I couldn't understand. I do now; it's the ink business over again."

"Ink?"

"Years ago I upset a bottle of red ink over some of father's documents and Nicky took the blame—he's always been like that with me. I think he's the only one of us with any capacity for love."

She sat on the sofa, her back to the window, and the pale-grey light put a faint halo round her auburn hair. An attractive woman in her prime, wife, mother and homemaker—the sort one sees pricing materials in a department store or discussing menus with a friend over coffee, a murderess three times over.

Wycliffe had seated himself in one of the wicker chairs which creaked with every movement he made. Time to direct the flow. In a conversational way he said, "It had all gone on for almost twenty years and there was no obvious reason why it shouldn't have gone on indefinitely, but something happened—something tripped the switch and released your pent-up hatred in three killings which were more like executions."

She made no protest but she got up from the sofa and moved slowly round the room until she reached the cupboards; there, with her back to him, she began to take out odd items and put them back again. She held up a little wooden cat. "That's Nicky's work—he used to do a lot of carving from odd bits of wood—he made a whole chess set; that must be here somewhere."

Wycliffe said, "When did Newcombe come to see you?"

She was silent for a moment or two and she didn't turn round, then she said, "Saturday it was—Saturday of last week, a week ago today. . . . The doorbell rang and I answered it and there he was. . . . I hadn't come face to face with him since before Esther was born."

She turned away from the cupboards and her features creased as though she would weep but she recovered. "I knew that he had changed, but I was shocked to see him; he was filthy—repellent! I could hardly bear to have him in the flat but it was that or talking to him on the doorstep where we might have been seen."

"What did he want?"

"In a word—money, but not from me; he wanted to threaten the family through me. He talked a lot about Esther being his child and made vague threats about going to law; he said that Ruby Price would have to back him up. . . . But all that wasn't the point. . . ."

"What was the point?"

She shivered. "I can't put it into words; it was partly his manner —intimate, smarmy and menacing . . . he was revolting! He even suggested . . . 'For old times' sake,' he said. I kept reminding myself that he really was Esther's father and it made me feel sick.

"I got rid of him somehow; I don't know what I said—what I promised, but when he had gone, although he hadn't touched me, I had a bath and I made up my mind to kill him."

She stopped speaking, her voice had failed her, and it was some time before she could carry on. "I knew that Nicholas had a pistol. Back in the early seventies Nicholas made up his mind that the country was going over to anarchy and that everybody must learn to defend themselves. He persuaded Maurice, Edward, me—and even little Esther, to learn to shoot. I quite enjoyed it; we used to practice on a target set up at the bottom of the lawn. Well, you know the rest . . . it was so easy, and I didn't feel anything. I certainly didn't feel that I had killed someone."

"Why did you search the cottage?"

"I didn't; I had a vague idea that by tumbling things about it would look as though someone had been after Emily's money— there's always talk in the village about Emily's money."

"And the photograph in the parlour?"

She understood at once. "I don't know—when I saw it it seemed to bring everything back. I snatched it off the wall and smashed it, then I took the photograph home and burnt it."

The creaking of Wycliffe's chair could be heard above the wind and the dull roar of the water. She reached into some hidden pocket and came out with cigarettes and a little lighter. She lit a cigarette and smoked in silence for a while.

"I didn't sleep much that night—not because I was worried or because I felt any sort of guilt—I was excited. For years I had been hemmed in—stifled, and suddenly I saw how I could be free. It was as though I had been shut up in a room for a long time and suddenly discovered that the door wasn't locked. . . . When I came back from the cottage I slipped the gun into one of the drawers in my bedroom. That night I got up to look at it—" She broke off, frowning. "It seems ridiculous, I know, but it was the way a child looks at a favourite teddy bear—a friend, but somehow more than a friend because it had magical powers." She turned to Wycliffe in sudden doubt, "You think I'm mad!"

"No."

"You can't possibly understand."

"I'm willing to try."

"I stood looking down at that pistol in the drawer; I touched it—stroked it. I was *comforted* by it."

Her eyes had taken on an inward look and she allowed her cigarette to smoulder between her fingers. "I thought a lot about Ruby Price that night. Until then I had always found her rather frightening. Some girls—Catholic girls—get a sort of crush on the Blessed Virgin; I never did; she always seemed to be *watching* and watching with a superior air. It was the same with Ruby Price, but that night I saw her as contemptible—she was nobody—*less* than nobody, for she was a kind of parasite, sucking away at other people's lives. . . . I don't remember deciding anything about her.

"It was very odd. At some time in the early afternoon—Monday afternoon—I was walking up through the churchyard with the pistol in my handbag. If someone had asked me where I was going, I should have answered, quite truthfully I think, that I didn't know, that I was out for a walk. . . . I took no precautions, I mean I made no effort not to be seen. It was a year or two since I'd been to see Ruby but nothing had changed. The back door was on the latch and Ruby was upstairs with the radio turned up to full volume; it was some sort of play. . . . I went in and up the stairs to her room. I was actually in the room looking at her—she was having tea—

before I took the pistol out of my bag; then I walked towards her with it in my hand. She looked up and saw me only when I was two or three feet from her. . . ."

She sighed deeply and her eyelids drooped; it looked almost as though she might fall asleep.

Wycliffe said, "You burned some of her envelopes."

She made a restless movement and opened her eyes. "Yes, I did. I took my time, looking around, and I found her *records*—all those envelopes with people's names on them. They disgusted me! To collect information about people like that is not only impertinent, it's indecent. I pushed some of them into the stove and set them alight. I didn't care if it burned the house down."

"The envelopes you burned were mainly concerned with your family."

"Probably. I suppose they were the ones which caught my eye but I didn't do it for any special reason. . . ."

"You didn't leave any prints—fingerprints."

"I didn't think about it. I was wearing gloves—I always wear gloves if I go out because my hands are so ugly. 'Your worst feature!' Mother used to say." She held them out. It was true, they were inclined to be red with rather thick, short fingers. "Mother used to call them 'washerwoman's hands.'

"I came back without bothering whether I was seen or not; it seemed that nothing could go wrong and I found it very difficult to behave normally so I pretended I had had too much to drink—which I often do." A sour little smile. "Of course I was excused from going down to dinner."

Her cigarette had burned itself down almost to her fingers; she dropped it on the floor and ground it out with her heel, then she looked up abruptly, "Do they shut you right away? In prison, I mean?"

"It depends on what sort of prison one is sent to."

"You think they will send me to some sort of prison for psychiatric cases. 'Detained at Her Majesty's Pleasure'—isn't that what they used to say? I can't see Her Majesty getting much pleasure out of me."

"A great deal has to happen before there is a question of sending you anywhere."

She smiled a bitter little smile. "You are like Father—it's not your department." She came back to the window and stood, looking out. "It's a wonderful view on a fine day—right down the valley. If the sun isn't shining in your eyes you can see the sea at Torbay. Mother used to take us there when we were children; she had an old Morris and we used to bundle in. . . ."

It was a bizarre situation; he had to remind himself that he was listening to a woman who would spend that night and succeeding nights in a police cell, charged with murder. The tale she was telling, shorn of nostalgic digressions, emasculated and formalized, would appear as a statement, typed by some two-fingered policeman. *"I raised the pistol and aimed at her head; I pulled the trigger. At the time I did not think about what I was doing. . . ."*

"Of course it didn't last—that feeling of excitement—euphoria, I think they call it. That night I woke up in a terrible state. I was scared. There was no way back and I kept saying to myself, 'As long as you live; as long as you live . . .' I got out of bed and looked at the pistol lying in my drawer and I almost decided to end it. . . . I don't know what stopped me."

She had her hands clasped tightly together and she was raising and lowering her arms from the elbows.

"I was better next day; almost back to normal."

She could not stay still; she walked over to the cupboards and stopped by the one with a false bottom. Using her fingernails, she lifted the loose board which one of Wycliffe's men had replaced.

"Of course you found this; I think I left it open. We used to call it Maurice's *Rudery* because he kept in there books we weren't supposed to read and pictures of naked girls. . . . It all seemed very wicked. . . . I put the things I took from Nicky's cupboard in there—except the pistol. That was how I got Frank to come down here last night, by saying I'd found those things. . . ."

She was silent for a long time; then, still with her back to him and speaking in a low voice, she said, "I had to do it. . . . What he did to me was despicable, and in all the years of our marriage he gave me nothing . . . nothing! It was his icy coldness; he always looked at me in that speculative way that he looked at a balance sheet or an estimate. . . . After Newcombe—after they found him he gradually began to suspect me. . . . He said nothing but he watched me —everything I did or said, waiting to catch me out. . . ." She drew a deep breath which was almost a sigh. "Then, on Friday morning— the morning of the fair, he came into my bedroom when he was getting ready to go to the office. He was wearing only his shirt and trousers, in the middle of dressing, and he stood there at the bottom of my bed, looking at me. I was only half awake at first.

"I don't know how long he stood there, just staring at me; he didn't say anything and I was frightened. . . . I knew then that I would have to go through with it."

She drew her cloak about her and shivered.

The wind had dropped and the rain had eased; in a few minutes they would be able to walk back to the house.

It was dark when he arrived home and Helen was watching the television news but she fussed over him and insisted on concocting a meal. He joined her in the kitchen and watched her at work. Normally he would have prepared the trolley, made the coffee, and been generally useful. . . . She had Gertrude's build, Gertrude's colouring—auburn hair without the freckles, and though she was a few years older, she did not look her age.

For days to come he would exist in two worlds, then the Beale images would gradually fade and he would be himself again. Until, with another case, he started to pick up the threads of yet other lives, lives of people of whom he had never heard.

Helen brought him back to earth. "What happened to my car?"

"Good grief! It's still on the Green at Washford."

She smiled. "Never mind; tomorrow is Sunday; we'll drive over, it will be a pleasant trip and if it's fine we can picnic on the moor."

It was more than a year after the Washford affair when Helen drew his attention to a report in the local paper of the marriage of "Miss Esther Vicary to her cousin, Mr. Edward Beale, both of Ashill, Washford. . . . The bride is the granddaughter of Mr. Simon Beale, chairman of Beales' Household Stores; the bridegroom is a

021

landscape painter whose work is in increasing demand. The couple are spending their honeymoon touring in France."

Helen said, "His father, and her mother; I wonder if they will have children."

Wycliffe sighed. His feelings were too complex to put into words and all he said was, "Life owes them something."

W. J. Burley is the author of many novels of mystery and suspense, including *Wycliffe's Wild Goose Chase*, *Wycliffe and the Scapegoat* and *Wycliffe in Paul's Court*, all published by the Crime Club. A graduate of Oxford, Mr. Burley lives in Cornwall, England.